Highlights

A Collection of Work

by

Attleborough Writers' Group

2011

Attleborough Writers' Group

The copyright of individual items remains with the author.

Published by
AWG Publishing
c/o 4 Albemarle Villas
London Road
Attleborough
Norfolk
NR17 2DD

Cover design by Sheila Charles
Internal illustrations by Enid Scoging and Rosemary Davis

Proofreading and typesetting by Wendy Fleckney
www.wordfocus.co.uk

Printed by
Copyzone Limited
Bishop's Stortford
Tel: 01279 657769
www.copyzone.co.uk

ISBN: 978-0-9564308-2-3

We gratefully acknowledge the grant given by Breckland Council.

Highlights

Contributors

Sheila Charles

Rosemary Davis

Deborah Dunseith

Margaret Dutton

Rosemary Ford

Hazel Gooderson

Enid Scoging

Iris Welford

INDEX

	Page
The Churchyard At Morwenstow – *Sheila Charles*	7
St Valentine's Bingo – *Enid Scoging*	10
Tears And Tiaras – *Deborah Dunseith*	11
Too Large – *Margaret Dutton*	13
Friends Forever – *Rosemary Ford*	15
What's That I Hear? – *Hazel Gooderson*	17
Water Shed – *Rosemary Davis*	20
Strutting The Boards – *Iris Welford*	21
Blind To The Help Of A Doctor – *Rosemary Davis*	23
Early Morning Walk – *Sheila Charles*	25
Weather For Jim – *Hazel Gooderson*	26
A Good Night Out – *Deborah Dunseith*	27
Question Time – *Margaret Dutton*	30
Back To Reality – *Iris Welford*	31
A Fine Day Out – *Rosemary Ford*	33
The Night That Changed My Life – *Hazel Gooderson*	35
Beside The Seaside – *Deborah Dunseith*	37
Too Large – *Enid Scoging*	39
Jealousy – *Sheila Charles*	42
Camping – *Rosemary Davis*	44
Hot And Cold – *Margaret Dutton*	45
A Day Out – *Hazel Gooderson*	49
Beware The Greeks! – *Enid Scoging*	51
Pitch Perfect – *Deborah Dunseith*	54
The Weather Forecast – *Iris Welford*	54
An Uplifting Example – *Sheila Charles*	55

	Page
Like Mother, Like Daughter – *Rosemary Ford*	57
Sunday Highlight – *Enid Scoging*	59
Grandma's Rules – *Iris Welford*	61
Winter's Edge – *Sheila Charles*	64
Christmas Tanka – *Rosemary Ford*	64
Here I Go Again – *Rosemary Davis*	65
Watershed – *Hazel Gooderson*	66
It's A Fake – *Margaret Dutton*	67
The Road to Maturity – *Rosemary Ford*	69
Think Of Me – *Deborah Dunseith*	72
The Ideal Parents – *Sheila Charles*	73
A Latin Encounter – *Iris Welford*	75
Fog – *Enid Scoging*	80
Moving The Summerhouse – *Hazel Gooderson*	81
Meantime – *Margaret Dutton*	83
Red Sea – *Rosemary Davis*	86
The Weatherman – *Iris Welford*	86
The She-Wolf – *Sheila Charles*	87
The Samovar – *Margaret Dutton*	91
His Sainted Mother – *Rosemary Ford*	95
A Social Gathering – *Enid Scoging*	97
Watershed – *Deborah Dunseith*	100
The Leopard-Skin Bird – *Hazel Gooderson*	101
Love In The Park – *Iris Welford*	103
Royal Wedding – *Margaret Dutton*	106
The Outing – *Enid Scoging*	107

	Page
Going Up In The World – *Sheila Charles*	109
Eclipse – *Rosemary Davis*	111
What Ye Sow – *Deborah Dunseith*	112
Lost – *Iris Welford*	113
Too Large – *Hazel Gooderson*	117
Winter Magic – *Enid Scoging*	119
Restless Legs – *Deborah Dunseith*	120
Hot Pickings – *Margaret Dutton*	121
A Day Out – *Enid Scoging*	123
An Uplifting Moment – *Rosemary Ford*	126
Sisterly Jealousy – *Hazel Gooderson*	127
Weather Or Not – *Rosemary Davis*	129
The Peep Show – *Sheila Charles*	131
Mother's Prayer – *Margaret Dutton*	134
Do You Fancy A Holiday – *Hazel Gooderson*	135
Watershed – *Iris Welford*	136
A Whole Lotto Luck – *Deborah Dunseith*	137
Wind – *Enid Scoging*	142
Welcome to Attleborough – *Rosemary Ford*	143

THE CHURCHYARD AT MORWENSTOW
Sheila Charles

The prevailing north-westerly blew with the most frightful force during the night, causing a terrific sea. The Caledonia rolled and pitched; frequently her decks were submerged. A heavy wave smashed against the fo'c'sle breaking several windows and flooding the seamen's quarters. Pillows were used to stop up the windows.

"Get to the rigging," the captain shouted, "or we'll all go down."

Another thunderous wave raged at the figurehead. Crashing on the deck, in seconds it split a lifeboat into driftwood, to be collected and used to build huts, repair roofs, keep the fires in, by Cornishmen from Sharpnose Point to Hartland. Seamen were unable to keep their feet, and those that had managed to climb the rigging could do little more than cling to it in the ferocity of the storm. The strain on the forward rigging proved too great and gave way.

The crack from the foremast was lost to the gale-force winds. It broke about ten feet above the deck, dragging with it the main topmast. As she fell the spars struck the wheelhouse. The wreckage was hurled from side to side in the punishing torrents, sweeping everything overboard as the deck railings gave way. In a few seconds the crew was depleted by three; the ship was heading towards the rugged shoreline. The captain, exhausted and uncertain of his position, tried to heave the vessel to. His gnarled features were highlighted by the moon, his gaze drawn to the jagged cliffs ahead and the white ruff of surf frothing at their feet. For the first time in his life he prayed – and then swore – as the ship was drawn onto the rocks.

"Every man for himself," he yelled as he jumped.

* * *

"Why are we going to Morwenstow?" asked Carne. They were trekking through moorland, edged by thorn bushes that had been moulded by unrelenting westerlies. While his father answered Carne's question they followed the narrow seaward path through fields to the remote Cornish village. They bought ice creams and then made their way to the churchyard, to find the Scottish girl in a tam-o'-shanter brandishing a cutlass. It was now time for Carne to learn some historical facts about the existence of Cornish folk; how church towers were used as beacons to warn passing ships of danger. Carne was intrigued by the facts, mixed with a few myths, that survival often depended on the salvage taken from wrecks.

"Over here Dad," called Carne, his angular outline highlighted by his sun-bleached hair, blowing like tufts of grass in the wind, as he ran towards the white painted figurehead that marks the burial place of The Caledonia's nine dead seamen. He stroked her enthusiastically, even though she looked rather menacing and weather-beaten: who wouldn't after being half buried in this exposed site for one hundred and sixty years?

They went inside the Norman Church to view the memorial stained glass window together, before they walked to the Point and descended the steep route down the cliff and onto Cotton Beach.

"A cargo of cotton would have made for rich pickings at one time you know?" said Carne's dad.

The shoreline revealed an untrodden repository of shipwreck atmosphere. The highlight being a six-foot anchor wedged among the rocks, boney-looking shackles and rusting chains, buried in sand.

"D'you think these are from The Caledonia, Dad?"

"Maybe." smiled his father.

"Did anyone survive?"

"Just one," his father answered, wistfully.

* * *

Staying at the Old Vicarage that night, Jack Curnow read Carne a shipwreck story and answered a lot more questions. Once downstairs Jack sat pondering over his day's explorations with his son, before settling down to read Jeremy Seal's *The Wreck at Sharpnose Point*, feeling satisfied that Carne had shown some enthusiasm about his family history. Tomorrow he would tell him more about his inheritance.

ST VALENTINE'S DAY BINGO
Enid Scoging

Held in the dining-room,
Warm and redolent of onions,
The round wooden tables
Stood grouped
With their red-cloth coverings,
Just three of them, clustered close.
Bright winter sunshine
Pierced dust-covered windows,
Throwing light on elderly faces,
Accenting furrowed and pallid skin.
Some patients sat on chairs
With broad supporting arms
And waterproof seats.
Some sat hunched in their wheelchairs.
And others steered their walking-frames
To the nearest point of rest.
At the caller's voice,
Relentlessly shrill,
They wielded their coloured felt pens.
"Two and one, twenty-one, key of the door."
None would ever be young again,
Nor have a key to their own front door.
Five assistants sat close by,
Guiding arthritic fingers
To colour the numbered squares.
"Two little ducks, twenty-two."
BINGO!
"Well done Mary!" She rose on shaky legs
To claim her prize – a packet of biscuits –
As her carer straightened the skirt
Caught in her knickers.

TEARS AND TIARAS
Deborah Dunseith

I got there three days early to guarantee a perfect view. I pitched my tent right next to a family of five from Attleborough who were later interviewed by *Look East* sitting in their Union Jack picnic chairs. The adults said that they wouldn't have missed it for the world, whilst the children complained that the constant whoosh of traffic and the chimes of Big Ben kept them awake at night. They all agreed however that it was tons better than being at school.

An air of excited anticipation greeted us on the morning of the big day. Bright and early, I brewed up a mug of Earl Grey, checked my dreadlocks and then carefully painted my face red, white and blue. I packed my belongings and took up prime position right next to the barriers draped in patriotic bunting and flags depicting the happy couple.

A bookmaker from Ladbrookes, very dapper in a grey morning suit and top hat, stood amongst the crowds. He hugged a huge blackboard showing odds on the colour of the Queen's hat. Black came in at one hundred to one, whilst yellow was a much safer bet and the odds-on favourite.

I saw a couple of teenage girls wearing sparkly tiaras and T-shirts saying 'Wills asked me first but I said no', which made me giggle. Countless stalls started to spring up selling everything from coronation chicken sandwiches and corgi-decorated cup-cakes to 'lay back and think of England' condoms! The *Big Issue* seller looked delighted as he was handed a £10 tip. "I love the Royals," he shouted. "Roll up and get your souvenir copy."

Suddenly the cheering throng surged forward, straining for snaps of the Royal procession. All at once there he was in the back of the chauffeur-driven Bentley. Prince William, resplendent in red military tunic, smiled and waved happily, to the delight of the crowd. The car seemed to slow as it came level with me. A beaming Prince Harry nudged his brother and excitedly they both gave me the thumbs up sign ... or did I imagine that?

A man bellowed from the crowd: "Diana would be proud." And I can say, as the tears rolled down my paint-streaked face, that I was.

TOO LARGE
Margaret Dutton

"Push! Come on, sweetheart, push!" The sweat ran down Jackie's back as she cradled the trembling young girl. "Once again, push," she encouraged, mopping the anxious face with cooling wipes.

The little lass started to cry and moan, and newly-qualified Jackie looked around for more help. She brushed the damp hair away from both their brows and said as brightly as she could, "Let's have one last big effort ... push!"

The young girl moaned, "Too big," and Jackie felt scared. This wasn't rocket science; it's happening all round the world but something was wrong, and both knew it. Jackie stood up and felt around. All seemed fine, she could do with back-up, but every member of staff was busy, and time was getting short.

"Hayley, I want you to give one almighty push when I say so. Ready? One, two, three ... PUSH!"

Hayley squeezed her face, panted, groaned, and yelled, "I can't do it," and tried to get up. "I want me mum!" she screamed, her eyes wide with terror.

"OK, take a deep breath; and again ... calm down, we'll try again in a few minutes, with just one more big push, you'll be there."

Jackie patted the trembling hand, wiped the hair away from the forget-me-not-blue eyes, and stretched her own aching back. The clock on the wall warned Jackie it was taking too long. Trying not to show her anxiety, she looked out of the window, and saw the girl's mum approaching. She went to the door, and beckoned her in. Hayley burst into more tears, and clung to her mother.

"I'm not big enough! I want to go home."

"I'm telling Hayley, with just one more push, we'll be fine, so all together now ... push!"

"Oh, for God's sake, don't they teach you anything about real life at your fancy colleges," snapped Mum. "Look, her foot is stuck and do you know why? She's wearing her brother's wellies that are too large for her. We stuffed them with newspaper so she could walk in them. The paper's got wet and swollen; take the paper out, and Bob's your uncle ... blockage over. You've got a lot to learn young woman!"

Mother and limping child left, and Jackie wished she had never stopped smoking.

FRIENDS FOREVER
Rosemary Ford

Brenda and Janet shared a room at The Beeches Residential Care Home. This suited them well enough as they had been friends for a long time; just about all their lives in fact.

They knew each other's moods and habits, and Brenda understood how Janet felt when her only son's long awaited visit lasted barely ten minutes, and Janet understood when Brenda's poor old feet hurt so much she got a bit tetchy and snapped at everyone. They knew not to mention certain things, like Brenda's husband Jack's terrible car crash, or Janet's daughter's cancer scare. But their salvation was that they knew how to make each other laugh. Janet only had to say the name 'Alfie' to Brenda in a certain deep, sexy voice, and they would both fall into fits of uncontrollable giggles at the memory of some otherwise long-forgotten boyfriend, even though they were both well into their seventies. 'I'd LOVE a Babycham' was another trigger for fits of uncontrollable laughter. It was better than crying …

Today though they could find nothing to laugh about. Mrs Snelgrove, the dragon in charge of the home, had waylaid them as they hobbled out of the dining room.

"Ah!" she said, false bonhomie oozing from her smile. "Just the two ladies I wanted to see. You know we are so popular at The Beeches that we have a waiting list. Do you remember when you first came, I said that your room was really meant for three people?"

"I don't remember that," said Janet with dignity. "I thought you said there used to be three people in there but there wasn't room to swing a cat …"

"Rubbish!" snapped the dragon. "And we mustn't forget that you do have the room at a reduced rate. Anyway, a very nice lady from the north of England is moving in this afternoon, so that's that."

It was no use arguing. Brenda and Janet were asked to fold away some of their clothes from the wardrobe and to clear some drawers, and the dragon and her helper sent them to wait downstairs while they manhandled the beds closer together, and just managed to get a third one squeezed in.

Brenda and Janet sat stiffly in the lounge awaiting the new arrival.

"We don't have to like her," said Brenda.

"We don't have to be too nice," said Janet. "It will never be the same again. Just being together was what made it bearable."

The door opened and the smiling dragon ushered in a nervous looking lady wearing a mauve coat.

"These are your kind new room mates," she boomed falsely. "Brenda Gates and Janet Carter. And this is Maureen Wilson, all the way from Whitley Bay."

Brenda and Janet looked at each other.

"It can't be …" said Brenda.

"It is! Maureen Lister you used to be, and you were at High Lane School with us!"

Maureen looked in disbelief for a few seconds, then a broad smile lit up her face.

"Brenda and Janet! I never forgot you when we moved away. Oh, and by the way, I'd love a Babycham…"

The three old friends fell into each other's arms, laughing and crying in equal measure.

WHAT'S THAT I HEAR?
Hazel Gooderson

Margery was returning from her walk with Oscar as the light started to go. It had been a beautiful spring day and the fading sun over the cliff-top was casting shimmers on the sea.

"Well Oscar, what do you think Dorothy has spent the day preparing for my dinner?"

At the sound of his name, the small brown and white Jack Russell turned from his seaweed foraging and put his head on one side. *Dinner?* That sounded hopeful, although he was enjoying himself here, in and out the caves, chasing wonderful smells and barking at the waves.

Margery had felt that she needed a break and whilst searching the internet one cold April afternoon for 'B&B – dogs welcome', she now found herself and Oscar at this delightful place.

The guest house was run by Mr and Mrs Tom Savage, but on Margery's first night nothing was too much trouble. *Call me Dorothy* had bustled back and forth throughout the meal checking Margery had enough of everything, and Oscar could have the lamb bone, and would she like the radio on, and would she care to join Tom and herself in their personal lounge for a chat by the log fire?

Margery had accepted the kind offer and learnt that Lighthouse Cottage shared its garden with the lighthouse, and Tom was the keeper. He regaled her with tales of the olden days when his work was demanding and the fishermen had been grateful for his light shining out as a welcome beacon after their night's work. The rocks were dangerous, lurking beneath the waves, and when the storms came, the wind would be desperate to drive the crafts towards their angry pinnacles.

In her room now, refreshed from the walk, Margery poured sherry into the bathroom glass and stood at the window sipping the amber liquid and gazing out to sea, delicious smells tempting her taste buds.

Twenty minutes later in the dining room, washed, changed, combed and lipstick-adorned, she was introduced to Sam and Nick, just starting their honeymoon after a low-budget wedding and a baby due soon, with no spare money for Caribbean celebrations or even photos, come to think of it.

Margery felt it was kinder for the young couple not to have her seventy-year-old presence and amused herself reading the guide book of the area: *It is hard for the visitor to imagine that this quiet sleepy hamlet was once a thriving town, rife with smuggling ...*

Lying in her bed, with Oscar snoring at her side, Margery counted the lighthouse flashes past her window and tried to imagine the contraband being smuggled ashore in days of old.

It was some time later that Margery was roused from a deep slumber by the growling grumble of Oscar.

"What's up boy?"

Oscar jumped onto the bed and burrowed under the covers. Shadows were cast on the bedroom wall as the light came and went on its journey of protection for weary travellers.

Margery strained her ears for whatever had disturbed her faithful companion, then slid out of bed and went across to the window. She tried to focus her ageing eyes on the scene. A figure was bending into the boot of a vehicle. What should she do? Bang on the glass and wave, go back to bed, ring the police? Her mind was too active after reading that book at dinner and there was nothing sinister. *Go back to bed old lady*, she told herself, *and don't be so nosy.*

The morning sun rising in the east woke Margery as the rays of light danced on the bedroom wall. Margery, clothed in dog-walking tracksuit, emerged quietly to the outside world for the benefit of Oscar. The gentle breeze lifted the sea air to their nostrils and, with tail up, Oscar was away along the cliff path chasing the night smells.

"Oh Margery, dear," the early risers were greeted with on their return, "did you hear anything in the night? When I came downstairs this morning, all the paintings and ornaments had gone!"

Now, here was a dilemma, what should she say? *Yes*, and be a witness who had done nothing, or *No*, and let that poor young couple have a start in life with the money from selling the treasures acquired by Tom and Dorothy over their years of contraband dealing?

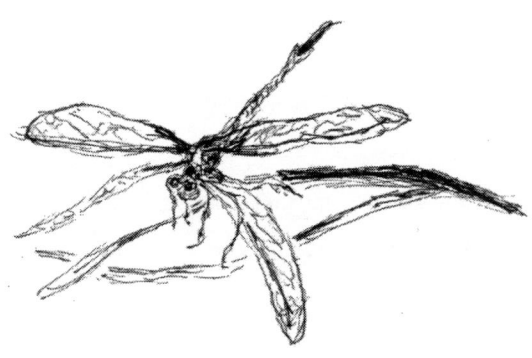

WATER SHED
Rosemary Davis

The water shed, the water shed.
Where in winter there's icicles
hanging above your head.
Your toes are numb and you dread
that icy drip above your head.

The water shed, the water shed.
Where in summer
a black spider spins its web
or runs across your leg.

The water shed, the water shed,
but you have to endure
with bare bum on seat
cringing with fear.

The water shed, the water shed.
At night it's worse, in the dark
with a candle that flickers,
as a draught threatens to plunge you
into a deeper chasm.

STRUTTING THE BOARDS
Iris Welford

Belle leaned as close to the mirror as she could and, with precision, painted large lips over her own with a bright red waxy lipstick. With a quick flick of her golden curls, she felt ready to perform her role as Cinderella. The dressing room door opened.

"The cat's disappeared. Is it in here?" Henry, the florid-faced Director, barked.

"No, I haven't seen it. What are you going to do? We can't start without the cat."

"I've sent Charlie round the Chinese Take-Away down the alley. Old Wang keeps a big orange thug called Fred, he'll have to do."

"How are we going to keep Fred on the stage – on a lead?"

"Don't be stupid, Belle, I'm putting down a sardine which will be hidden under your skirt when you're sat on the floor. I'm sorry, you're going to smell fishy, but the punters will think Fred is nudging you. Don't pick him up because he bites."

"This is all I need," Belle sighed like a true performer. "Good job the first scene is short."

The bell rang indicating two minutes to curtain up. Belle took her place on the floor in front of the fire. By her side Fred was engrossed in his fishy supper, whilst in the wings Buttons was waiting for his entrance.

The curtain went up and the lights dimmed.

"Oh Tiddles," Cinders sighed, "will I ever be able to go to a ball like my sisters?" Fred munched noisily. "You and Buttons are my only friends," she said appearing to stroke Fred's back. Buttons entered to loud applause at which Fred took fright. He ran off the stage and jumped into the orchestra pit to the delight of the audience.

Meanwhile, under the stage, the real Tiddles was on the scent of something large. He had inspected most of the dark, murky, cobwebbed corners and was now heading to the middle of the room where various cardboard boxes stood. Above him he heard the heavy footsteps of the players and the audience clapping, but none of this deterred him from his mission.

Suddenly, something in the far corner stirred. A long dark figure approached him. "A rat," Tiddles thought, but then he realised the rat was Fred, the bully from down the road. Over the last few weeks there had been several showdowns but the outcome was always the same – Tiddles came off worse.

This time, Tiddles stood his ground as Fred came snarling towards him. Back arched and spitting, Fred's orange eyes glittered in the dark. Tiddles looked around for an escape but all he could see was a rope and a large shelf. Fred was now near enough for Tiddles to smell his fishy breath. Taking a flying leap on to the rope, Tiddles swung briefly back and forward and landed on the shelf. Fred followed. Suddenly, without warning, the trap-door above them opened and they were propelled on to the centre stage. Fred, oblivious to the cheering and applause, set about attacking Tiddles. Together they chased backwards and forwards across the stage. Buttons tried to catch Tiddles whilst Cinders chased Fred with her broom. The audience was delighted with these antics, but in the wings Henry was screaming, "Get the curtain down!"

The next day in the local paper a review said: "The opening scene of the drama society's *Cinderella* was the best I've seen in years – thoroughly recommended as fun for all the family." The problem was neither Tiddles nor Fred could be found for the next performance.

☙ ❧

BLIND TO THE HELP OF A DOCTOR
Rosemary Davis

Jenny sits on one side of the table; the only other furniture in this white-washed room is an easel with a whiteboard. A man sits on the other side, he's leaning forward, chin in the palm of his hand, fingers bent. With his eyebrows folded down, his eyes look at her intently. As he turns another card over he notes she's trying to imitate his look so he allows a small smile to creep into his eyes. To this she scowls up her face. He turns another over.

Each day Jenny is taken for a walk in the garden. The first week she could only see the black tarmac path, then the grain in the wood of the bench and the hand of the orderly who sits next to her. In the session with Dr Matthews, Jenny slowly starts to react.

"That looks like a bird, that like a fish."

Each time she names one, he attaches it to the whiteboard. As she starts to enjoy herself, her sense of humour starts to show.

"That looks like a two-headed pig, that looks like you."

Smiling, he joins in with the jokes. After six months of half an hour sessions and walks, Jenny finds the trees and the colours in the flowers that had been lost to her for so long.

Back in the white room, Dr Matthews turns the next ink blot over, her face brightens into wonder.

"That looks like my birthday cake, it has six candles."

His eyes change a little as he sees another barrier come down. This is something personal. He slips a photo out of a green folder – it's of a man. She stiffens, stating: "No." He immediately covers it with his big hand, kicking himself because it could be too soon, saying, "That's all right Jenny, it's just a photo, he can't hurt you."

She reacts, "Cake. Mummy's cake. I want Mummy."

As she leans forward, wiping all the cards onto the floor, crashing her chair over, she flees to the corner to become a ball of sobbing humanity. He rises, walks over and with the orderly's help coaxes her back to her feet saying, "That's all for today Jenny, I'll see you tomorrow."

From then on Jenny starts to tell Dr Matthews all about the night, ten years ago. When she was six, the banging that woke her. Of slipping out of bed and looking over the banisters. Seeing a man hitting Mummy with the iron that she was using to iron her school uniform. Blood spraying up the wall and of how she ran to hide in the cupboard. Also of her neighbour, Mary, coming round for a cup of tea and discovering the body, and about being found by the nice white angel, who she found out was one of the forensic team working on the case.

Forensics found minute pieces of flesh adhered to what had been a hot iron. Then matched it to her father's DNA.

He had lied to her over the years, twisting her mind and her memories.

Slowly, slowly, Dr Matthews unravelled fact from fiction and got to understand her manic depression. Helping her to crawl out of the dark tunnel and into the light. To build her confidence so she could finally go out and meet people, to study and to get a job working for him, Dr Matthews.

EARLY MORNING WALK
Sheila Charles

The light breeze from yesterday had changed to an icy blast and the mouse-grey clouds in the distance threatened a downpour. As Fred continued down the road it started to drizzle. "Just my luck!" he thought to himself. "September not yet over and winter starting already. No chance of staying out for long today."

He quickened his step, turning into the loke. He hadn't dared venture this way since that large rat had tried to attack Robin. But it provided more shelter and he could let Mickey have a bit more freedom. He must watch out for the barn owl here; it usually came this way first thing. He walked quietly, listening, and peering up at the sky through the branches. Mickey was content to keep his nose to the ground, moving about in zig-zag fashion. He kept one eye on him and one out for the barn owl.

Something brushed his cheek, startling him: more like a cobweb than a twig. He heard a rustle and a squeal from the undergrowth. Mickey limped out from the bushes and he stopped him with his foot. Mickey held up a paw as if to have it looked at but then Fred noticed the fresh blood oozing from his neck. Surely not again! It can't happen again. First he'd lost Wriggles – ran straight into the path of a plough – and shortly afterwards Scamp had disappeared down a rabbit hole. He thought it was unfortunate that Malvolio had died only minutes after bringing him home. He couldn't face much more loss at the moment.

A flash of white distracted Fred as the barn owl hovered above them. He watched it entranced, and in that moment Mickey darted off. Fred, furious, scoured the thicket; ah yes, over there. He held his breath and waited. Then he pounced, pinning the mouse under his snow white paws and drooling in anticipation of the kill. Fred knew playtime was over,

"Goodbye Mickey, nice playing with you. MEOW!"

WEATHER – FOR JIM
Hazel Gooderson

The weather forecast for the East of England.

The day will start dry with blue sky and sunshine, but a band of low pressure will bring in a bank of cloud and rain.

Strong winds will bring cooler weather and temperatures will drop to below average for the time of year.

By mid-afternoon the rain will have set in.

An end to weeks of dry weather in East Anglia.

Here comes summer!

A GOOD NIGHT OUT
Deborah Dunseith

Donna fell through the door of the school hall, narrowly missing a parked buggy. Looking completely flustered, she took a moment to gather herself before scanning the room to find me. I waved and she waved back.

"Sorry I'm late, hun," she boomed, throwing down her handbag and slipping effortlessly into the tiny chair. Her thick dark hair stuck up in a bun seemed to be collapsing like the Leaning Tower of Pisa. She wore no make-up save the merest hint of lip gloss. She hadn't bothered much since the divorce, I thought to myself.

"Where are the others?" I asked trying to keep the annoyance from my voice.

"Not coming."

"What?" I gasped.

"Don't tell me you're surprised?" my friend continued. "There's only so many things you can do with a wooden spoon and we've had it four times on the trot."

"Well," I snapped, "they won't let us play with just two people will they? And that bumps up the price of the entry fee for us."

"Don't worry," Donna stroked my arm, "I've asked for reinforcements."

Before I had a chance to question, Donna was on her feet and smiling at a man fast approaching our table. "Hello," she beamed at the tall, greying, handsome stranger, "I'm Donna and this is Lesley. We always come and try to raise some much needed cash for the school, don't we Les?"

"Ladies, Adam Good at your service." Adam bowed and Donna giggled.

"Ooooh, do sit down Adam. What's your specialist subject?"

Adam's blue eyes twinkled. "Well I'd be rather embarrassed if I got any of the medical questions wrong, I've just joined the village practice."

"A doctor," I declared, stating the obvious.

"How rude of me," Adam went on, "I haven't offered you ladies a drink."

"Mine's a lager shandy and Les will have a ..."

"A lemonade," I interrupted. "I'm driving."

"Coming right up." Adam rose, slapped his back pocket and headed for the drinks table.

"Phwoar! I bet he's got a GOOD bedside manner," Donna enthused. "I can feel one of my chests coming on. Do you think he will examine me?"

I managed a weak smile.

"Ooooh, he's gorgeous ... here he comes now. Oh, GOODY, GOODY." Donna clapped her hands together with glee.

Dizzy Donna spent the rest of the evening drooling over Adam and it seemed to me that the doctor was quite taken with her. I began to feel very plain and my usual sparkling wit seemed to evaporate into thin air. At one point their hands briefly met whilst handing over the pencil for the sports round. Donna blushed and giggled like a school girl. "Oh grow up," I thought, highly irritated.

"I'm going to text Gary," I announced, "and check on the kids." But the pair didn't even notice as I reached into my bag for my mobile. To say I felt like a gooseberry was the understatement of the year.

Amazingly I felt a sense of relief going up to collect the wooden spoon. At least it signalled the end of a very difficult evening. The Governors had won again and were politely shaking hands. "It's not bloody *Mastermind*," I seethed as I flounced past their table.

But where were Donna and Adam? They were nowhere to be seen. How rude to leave without saying goodbye. I fumed all the way back to the car.

* * *

Gary was in the kitchen making a cup of tea when I arrived home. He greeted me with a kiss and nodded toward the dresser. The four other wooden spoons complete with happy felt-tip faces were standing stiffly, grinning at me. They were ready to meet the newest member of their family. I stuck my tongue out at them and yanked number five out of my bag.

Just then my mobile bleeped. It was a text message from Donna: **"Just having a lie down ... doctor's orders xx."**

QUESTION TIME
Margaret Dutton

Is there someone else?
I asked Narcissus.
Just us, he smiled,
his face reflected in my tears.

Did you eat the potatoes?
I asked Vincent.
No – sunflowers and ears of corn
became my watershed.

Were you homesick?
I asked Pocahontas.
As a fish on the moon
despite society's va-va-voom.

Was the Earth really blue?
I asked Neil.
I never looked; the stars and stripes
had to be held straight.

Do you have nightmares?
I asked Munch.
Only when I have too much
raspberry ice-cream.

Do you believe in God?
I asked Darwin.
There's a God in every battle trench,
… or so I've been told.

BACK TO REALITY
Iris Welford

My batteries were recharged after a summer of wall-to-wall sunshine but, as always, I steeled myself as I joined the others in the master's study. Teachers and staff were gathered in the oak-panelled room, helping themselves to coffee from the Thermos flasks and chatting merrily. Joan Grimshaw walked towards me sporting a deep tan.

"Did you enjoy the summer?" she asked. "I went sailing and spent two weeks on the Riviera. I suppose you went to Broadstairs again?" She raised her voice so that those nearby turned their heads towards us.

"Well, no, actually I didn't. My friend Tom and I went walking in the Dales and then went off to Portugal to stay in his apartment." I managed to raise my volume making sure I could be heard above the general din.

Joan's face fell, and I mean to the floor. Her ruby-red mouth gaped open showing her pink tongue, and her eyes opened wide. My hand went to my mouth as I stifled a giggle – she reminded me of *The Scream* by Munch – and coughed instead.

"I suppose Tom is some sort of relation is he? I haven't heard you mention him before." She sort of sniffed this comment to show her disapproval. "Or did you meet him on the internet?" Thinking this was funny she laughed loudly.

I put on my disdainful look and knitted my eyebrows together. "Actually Joan, Tom is an old friend from university, not that it's any of your business. He has just returned to this country having finished his posting to the ambassador in Brazil. But about your summer, Joan? Did you spend it with your mother again? Two weeks in the Riviera on a caravan park?"

I bristled as Joan pulled her shoulders back and straightened her spine trying to make herself taller than me. We stood like warriors anticipating who was going to make the first move when a tinkling bell called us all to attention.

The master, George Mitchell, brought the gaggle to order and instructed us to sit. George was a heavily-set man, with greying hair. With his legs outstretched as if he was in a gentlemen's club, he puffed on a fat cigar blowing out clouds of billowing smoke. In his left hand he held a whisky tumbler, a quarter full of the brown liquid even though it was only ten a.m.

"Welcome back, I hope you're all eager to start the new year." George's tone was dull and lifeless. "We have two new members of staff: Mr Parsons who will be teaching maths and Mrs Grady who will be taking over English whilst Miss Smith is away on maternity." George indicated that Mr Parsons and Mrs Grady stand. All eyes turned in their direction. "Thank you, be seated. We have a full intake, but be warned, some of the new kids have severe social problems. I advise you that slapping, punching, kicking and otherwise chastising the monsters will no longer be tolerated. No more breaking bones. I'm afraid your task of keeping order will be much harder."

There was a deadly silence. I looked at the newcomers and saw shock and disbelief on their faces as they fidgeted on their chairs.

"So, my friends, enjoy the coming weeks and we'll meet again before half-term. Refer any questions to my deputy." George stubbed out his cigar and made for the door, glass clenched in hand.

"Here we go again," I mumbled under my breath.

A FINE DAY OUT
Rosemary Ford

The long awaited day out went wrong right from the beginning. It was a Tuesday – Bin Day – and this led to an argument about whether it was Green Bin Day or Black Bin Day. In the end it didn't matter that Jill was right and Pete was wrong, because the refuse lorry slipped ever-so-quietly along the road before either bin was out.

"Oh well, don't worry," said Jill. "It wasn't full anyway. We don't get so much rubbish now it's just the two of us, so let's forget about it and go off for the day like we planned."

Pete looked at the sky. "Are you sure you want to go out? Looks like rain to me …"

"Yes I'm sure. And if it rains we can always go and have a long, lazy lunch somewhere or … or … go to the cinema."

Pete was unsure what to wear. "It depends on where we go, and you can't seem to make up your mind. One minute you want to go to the seaside and next minute to the Garden Centre and then it's go to Norwich and have a look round the shops and then go and visit Bill and Helen."

"Oh, for goodness sake, just wear what they call 'smart casual', and put a jacket and a spare pair of shoes in the boot with the umbrellas. What makes you think anyone will worry what we are wearing? Honestly, you make such a fuss. I've been ready for ages, and cleared up the breakfast things."

They bickered on for a bit, then grinned at each other and decided it was still a good idea to have a day out.

There was a bit of a hiccup when the car was reluctant to start, then it needed filling up at the garage. The price of the petrol made Pete suck his teeth in dismay and begin muttering about just going to Wymondham and back. Jill's riposte was to say that she had spent thirty years working in Wymondham and knew every inch of the place.

"I'd rather stay at home than go there," she snapped. "What would you say if I said to you, 'Let's just go to Banham'? You'd say I used to work there and it's the last place I would want to go."

"Well, now you mention it, I would quite like to go and see my old mates again …" replied Pete, but looking at Jill's face he added quickly, "But let's just get in the car and see where we end up."

Jill sat grim-faced as they headed along the A11. Soon they followed the Yarmouth road and she felt a minor thrill of excitement as she remembered how she had loved Yarmouth as a child.

It was March, so there was no problem parking when they arrived. They walked along the promenade in fitful sunshine and a brisk breeze. Jill wished she had worn more comfortable shoes, but kept quiet because Pete had warned her that sling-backs were not suitable. He strode on, looking to neither left nor right.

"Nice view," said Jill. "Shall we go and have a coffee? It's a bit breezy …"

"Coffee? We only just got here …" But they stopped at one of the few cafés that were open and had weak coffee before setting off again.

They had not gone far before the rain came. Not just a few spots but a real downpour. They sheltered in a doorway for a bit. Cinema? Too far away, they would be wet all day. Lunch? No decent place within walking distance. But the car was quite close, and HOME seemed very tempting …

Back home, they enjoyed their fish and chips from the shop nearby.

"What a lovely day out," smiled Jill. "We must do it again soon."

꙳ ꙳

THE NIGHT THAT CHANGED MY LIFE
Hazel Gooderson

I want to look but he says I shouldn't.

It began all those years ago at uni when I saw her on the catwalk in a different light. Wow, what a vision of perfection. After that show, I thought I had better Google her surname because I knew my family would expect some details if I pursued this beauty.

On Friday morning, 29th April 2011, the sun shone through the gap in my bedroom curtains, which was a good sign as Dad was letting me borrow his open-top car. After breakfast, I checked it for little brother's intervention – wouldn't surprise me what that boy did. He made sure I had one hell of a hangover after the stag-do.

It had been decided that I would wear the Irish Guards' uniform and so I began the long process of getting dressed. I think the bright red should look quite stunning for the photos and Grandma's yellow will look good with the pageboys. It's a shame Great Gran did not meet Kate.

We had had the TV on earlier, and with all the crowds lining the streets I knew that I would be expected to do lots of waving on the drive to the Abbey. I thought of Mum then, and how she had taught us to wave to the crowds all those years ago. I know she would have liked my fiancée.

"Ready for this?" Harry asks me above the ringing out of the bells. Imagine if I said no!

We remove our hats and smooth our hair. I know people comment on our different styles and colour. Not yet thirty and my hair is receding. I love Kate's. I wonder how she is?

The carefully selected floral arrangements were amazing at the dress rehearsal but today I notice their smells are mingled with the guests' perfumes as little bro' and I walk down the red carpet.

We are ushered out of the side chapel to stand at the altar and wait. The music we were guided to choose – Hubert Parry's *I Was Glad* – has started, and this is it. Beside me, Harry has seen her and is grinning. I've heard it said that your face gets fixed in a grin on your wedding day. My heart is pounding. I am so excited.

I turn to look. And there she stands. Veiled in ivory lace.

"You look beautiful," I say to Kate.

The Archbishop of Canterbury stands before us and proceeds with the ceremony.

It's a bit of a struggle to get that ring of Welsh gold on, but there, it's on and we are pronounced 'man and wife'.

BESIDE THE SEASIDE
Deborah Dunseith

Beryl thought that a beach hut was a bit of strange place for a blind date, but, as her friends had pointed out, anyone who owns a beach hut these days is doing OK for themselves. She supposed this was right and anyway the date would be conducted in broad daylight and in a very public place.

Beryl didn't realise though that the rendezvous hut would be right in the middle of a freshly painted row. To get there meant she had to traipse over the beach. The pebbles played havoc with her new stilettos. Turning her ankle for the fourth time she eventually stumbled across beach hut number twenty-three. The door was open and there were signs of life from within.

Beryl coughed nervously into her hand. Tommy Taverner turned slowly to look at his blind date.

"Blimey love, you scrub up well," he said looking Beryl up and down and licking his lips.

Instantly, Beryl knew she'd made a terrible mistake.

"Come on in," he continued, "I've made an effort babes. Wanna fish paste sarnie?" The kettle whistled on the camp stove and Tommy busied himself with the tea pot. "No mod cons 'ere darlin', if ya need a piss ya gotta go in the sea."

Before she had time to react, Tommy threw back his head and laughed so loudly that his yellow teeth seemed to shake in his head. He was a huge hulk of a man, sweating and sunburnt. As he laughed, his bulging stomach struggled to free itself from the confines of an ill-fitting dingy grey string vest. Suddenly his large hairy navel popped through one of the holes making Beryl gasp in horror. This was certainly not the smartly dressed, distinguished looking man she'd contacted via 'Silver Dreams', the online dating agency for the over sixty-fives. She felt thoroughly deflated. He'd probably used a photo of his son to lure his prey. What a rotter!

"Want sugar love?" Tommy continued. "Or are ya sweet enough?"

Beryl started to think about an exit strategy.

"Take a pew," ordered Tommy nodding towards a blue and white striped deckchair.

Beryl grimly obeyed. He had the sort of voice that meant he wouldn't take no for an answer. Tommy passed a mug of what looked like dishwater and Beryl noticed 'Jeanie forever' tattooed on his forearm. Beryl silently empathised with Jeanie.

"Just borrowed 'er for the day off me best mate 'Arry," Tommy said smugly, looking lovingly around the pristine beach hut and dunking his sandwich into his tea.

Beryl sighed. The last glimmer of happy-ever-after ebbed away with the tide. Thinking about the photo on the website she suspected the beach hut wasn't the only thing he'd 'borrowed off' good old 'Arry.

Just then a rather tubby, red-faced child rushed into the hut. Tears streamed down his fat little cheeks.

"Have you seen my dog?" he blurted out. "My dad let him off the lead and now he's run away."

"Nah mate," Tommy replied slurping his tea. "Beat it kid."

Beryl struggled out of the deckchair which seemed to be keeping her prisoner against her will. "I'll help," she cried, leading the distraught youngster smartly out of the hut.

Without looking back, Beryl kicked off her heels and ran for her life.

~ ~

TOO LARGE
Enid Scoging

Standing on the narrow path which separated his allotment from Sid's, Jack Stonely breathed out a very contented sigh. The warm summer evening made everything worthwhile. He straightened his aching back and smiled.

"Just look at your onions, Jack!" Sid's admiring comment broke into his thoughts. "How do you do it?"

"Just pee on the compost, Sid. Save it up. Don't waste it down the lav."

Sid laughed out loud. "You know my dad told me that one. Reckon it must work. Your veggies are great. Entering the Show this year?"

"Of course. I mean to win the Cup this time round."

"What do you do with all the extra? You and Rosa can't eat it all, surely?"

"Well, I give a lot away – to our kids of course; sell some from the stall by our front gate. Then we freeze quite a bit. But looking at all this I think we'll have to invest in a bigger freezer."

"Good luck at the Show, Jack," Sid wished him as he turned back to his rows of runner beans and his compost heap.

Walking back to their cottage, Jack's thoughts turned to the idea of buying a new chest freezer. Their current one was getting on – made funny noises and tended to leak over the kitchen floor, usually when they were away from home. He pushed open the back door.

"I'm back, Rosa," he called. He could smell cooking. Delicious savoury aromas were drifting from the kitchen. His wife looked up as he appeared in the doorway. "I've been thinking ..."

"Not again."

"Yes dear, important thinking. We need a new freezer. There's so much on the allotment ready for picking and our little old one ..."

"Very old one," reminded his wife.

"... needs replacing to cope with all the extra," finished her husband.

"A bigger one will be expensive," said Rosa as she licked the cake mixture from the wooden spoon.

"We can afford it," reassured Jack. "Tomorrow I'll go to Stephens' Electricals and have a look."

"I'll come with you!"

"Not until I've had a chat with them – get some brochures and a quote. Then we can decide."

"OK, dear. I've got things to do tomorrow. Paul and Alice are coming at the weekend, remember."

Jack stood in the middle of Stephens' Electricals, looking around at the gleaming white items. Sleek fridges, solid washing machines, tumble-driers, microwaves were all lined up in neat rows with colourful price cards firmly fixed, enticing shoppers to 'buy while stocks last'.

An assistant approached. "May I help you, sir?"

"Yes," said a bewildered Jack. "We need a new freezer – I'm just looking."

"What size, sir? We have a wide range in stock at the moment."

"Not quite sure, but we have so much from the allotment this year. Mustn't waste it."

"How about this one, sir? It has been reduced – a real bargain – and last in the line. Will it fit into your space?"

Jack ran his hands over the top of the gleaming white Iceking. He lifted the lid and peered inside. So much space – and at a bargain price.

"Just the job," he decided. "Can you deliver it?"

"Of course, sir. Shall we arrange a date?"

"Jack, how do you know if it will fit?" His wife's voice rose several decibels. "Did you take any measurements?"

"I'm good at that, Rosa. Remember I am a carpenter. I do lots of measuring."

The door-bell trilled and Jack walked along the hallway to open the front door.

"Afternoon, sir. Stephens' Electricals with your new freezer. Where do you want it?"

"In here," replied Jack and he stood back as the two men tried to negotiate the doorway.

"Too large," they announced in one voice. "Can't get it round the corner."

Rosa appeared behind Jack. "I knew it. You didn't bother to measure, did you? Now what are we going to do? It'll have to go back." Her exasperated voice was shrill and accusing.

"It will have to go in the shed," decided Jack. And that meant a walk behind old Bob's cottage, crossing the shared shingle pathway and a tricky manoeuvre alongside the adjoining hedge. The two delivery men rolled their eyes heavenwards as they humped and bumped the brand-new shiny white chest freezer towards Jack's shed.

"Just one question, sir," asked one of them. "Have you got any electricity in your shed?"

JEALOUSY
Sheila Charles

They call me the green-eyed monster, but in truth, I cannot see.
I simply feel my way about and listen carefully
to find out where there's room for me, dark corners suit me fine,
damp crevices provide me with a place to twist the mind.
I lurk amongst the shadows until love casts her spell,
engaging passion's fatal charm to blur my vicious smell.
Invasion is my forte, surrounding hope with doubt,
degrading trust and confidence is what I'm all about.

They say I'm a green-eyed monster, but in truth, I am not green.
I've got no skin to colour, in fact, I can't be seen.
I float around the world, I was banished long ago,
With sloth, and pride, and gluttony, wrath, greed, and lust, you know.
These others, I too hate and fear,
they make me shrink when they come near,
But I am fun and like to play,
and entertain myself this way.

They say I'm a green-eyed monster, but forsooth, it's just a scam.
I am not real, I don't exist as woman, child or man.
This image just a metaphor that Shakespeare brought to life
to help him set the scene to kill Othello's lovely wife.
He'd witnessed love's strange twists and turns
and understood the pain that burns
as love is soured and dreams consumed
when I project that fatal wound.

Say goodbye then to this 'creature' and accept me as I am.
A thing that has great power, to affect woman, child and man.
Destroying love and friendship with the feelings that pour out
in toxic words and actions, like poison from a spout.
Once you understand, that it's you creates the strife,
that wounds your love, and has the power to terminate a life,
you'll maybe take some action to try to calm your mind,
and leave the 'green-eyed monster' for someone else to find!

ಌ ✑

CAMPING
Rosemary Davis

The water-shed wasn't a shed any more, it was a smart yellow brick building with a red tiled roof. Inside it had showers, WCs, hand-basins and big butler sinks, all in brown and white.

Our tent was more like a shed. We had borrowed it from a friend who had acquired it some years before from the army. It was designed to sleep six men with sleeping bags. Not a mum, a dad and four lively young children with mattresses. However, by piling them at one end in the day and laying them all over the floor at night, we managed.

The weather was warm but it rained for the first two days, so on went the swim suits, Wellington boots and plastic see-though rain macs. John was all right, inside with his new paper. The children were having a high old time, running in and out of muddy puddles and playing hide-and-seek between the other tents and caravans. For me, it wasn't so good, trying to cook on a two-ring camping stove that had seen better days, wearing my bikini, with an umbrella over my head. Thank God I'd had the foresight to cook a big hock of bacon before going there.

To keep the flies off, I placed one of our folding chairs at the back of the tent with the joint on the seat and a sheet wrapped securely round it. I felt it would be quite safe. On the second night the rain stopped and I was enjoying the peace and quiet, then came a rustling. I got out of bed saying, "John someone's trying to steal our bacon."

I go left, he goes right, meeting at the tumbled-over chair, as an enormous hedgehog makes his escape.

HOT AND COLD
Margaret Dutton

Sweet, sweet irony. The hottest day of the year and I was having extra loft insulation laid, and an Aga fitted into my kitchen. The men hauling both cooker and combi-rolls were sweating like defeated Grand National horses. Quaffing my homemade lemonade, they watched as the TV weatherman forecast even hotter days ahead, with no sign of rain.

"Right, lads, let's get a move on. This lady's obviously going to need all this extra heat," they laughed, but I didn't.

I had moved in twelve months earlier, a retirement dream come true. Country village life, sadly alone now Jim had died, but I had time to do my pottery, have friends to visit this lovely part of Norfolk, and, as my sons insisted, 're-invent' myself. Except for the perpetual, numbing cold in the cottage all would have been bliss. No matter how many logs went on the fire, or how high the central heating thermostat was set, the chill in the cottage never went. It was costing me a small fortune; I cancelled a couple of holiday trips because my budget was so stretched just keeping warm.

I had a check-up with my GP, in case there was some health reason. He gently laughed, said I was tickety-boo, and hoped I was not being cold-shouldered by the village.

"Far from it," I replied. "They have given me a very warm welcome." Indeed, everyone else's house was blissfully warm, but visitors and family started to call me a skinflint for not having the heating on.

We had a beautiful spring, and sitting outside feeling the warm sun on my face and watching an early butterfly basking on my clay-lump walls, I decided to take matters to hand. So a reconditioned bright red Aga, and the thickest, most expensive loft insulation were being installed as the June temperature soared to 32C.

"Loft all cleared, Mrs. Jacques?" asked the cheerful boss as he hauled another roll of insulation into the hall.

"Yes, it was cleared before I moved in, and I've deliberately not put anything up there; as you get older it pays not to make things difficult."

I felt so guilty watching this band of workmen sweating in the heat, and when I told them the cottage was always so cold, they laughed and said, "We're not complaining, love, we can warm up outside!"

Suddenly, Craig, the skinny 'apprentice insulator', came running out of the cottage and was sick all over my hollyhocks. "I ain't goin' back insoide!" he announced to his boss, shaking like a leaf. The boss told me we had a problem. A big problem. They'd found two sets of bones tucked away under a partition in the roof. He had to inform the police, who had to inform the Coroner, and all work had to stop.

"Perhaps it's animal bones?" I asked timorously. "Squirrels, cats?"

"Animals don't wrap themselves in sacking," replied the frustrated boss. "The fuzz will make this a crime scene, so God alone knows when we can get back in and finish the job."

The heatwave continued as I was forced to spend the next three nights in 'The George and Dragon' whilst the police, crime scene investigators, etc., searched my cottage. I slept under just a sheet – not a fourteen tog duvet – welcoming the wafts of air from, joy of joys, an open window, thanking every cloud for having a silver lining. The police reported solemnly that the remains of two children had been discovered, and further investigations were taking place.

The pub landlord of my temporary home introduced me to 'Phil the Ferret' and we ate the pub's famous fish pie as Phil, the local historian – 'entirely amateur' – told me my cottage had once been two dwellings. They'd been part of Lord Sheridan's estate, long since gone. Over a carafe of chilled white wine, Phil said he had researched the families who'd lived in my cottage. He could go back to 1801 with certainty because of the Census. My cottage was a tied cottage for the estate farm labourers. In 1831 the local Assize Court tried Jacob Brown for stealing six turnips from his employer's field, and sentenced him to seven years' transportation. This was a time of great social unrest due to the Enclosures Act, with poor harvests two years running, and the Swing Riots after farm labourers' wages were cut. Jacob Brown lived in my cottage. The records showed he had lost a leg in an 'agricultural' accident, and then lost his job. Phil produced the transportation lists for 1832, and Jacob Brown of this parish had sailed to New South Wales, Australia, and was never heard of again.

"The children – his children – are they the little bones we found?"

"He had two young children according to the Census of 1831, and a wife, Eliza. There's an eviction notice dated December 1831, removing her from your cottage. But no record of any of them after that. It was a bitter winter that year, the river froze for months, drifting snow made it impossible to walk anywhere. The workhouse was twelve miles away, how could she get there? Pitiable and so unjust."

The police reported that the remains were of two children, very malnourished, but uninjured, and had been hidden in my cottage roof for over one hundred and fifty years. It was impossible to establish a cause of death, most likely starvation, but both children had been lovingly wrapped in flour bags and sacking after their deaths.

"Can I bury them?" I asked, "With a proper funeral?" The authorities agreed, and after all the formalities, on a bright warm autumn day, the two little bodies were laid to rest, mourned by our entire village, the school children dropping wheat and corn ears into their grave.

Returning home, I opened my door, and my cottage was warm for the very first time.

A DAY OUT
Hazel Gooderson

"Sophie, hi, it's Georgia. Are you free on Thursday the 16th? Desmond has given me two day-tickets for the Health Spa that recently opened in the next town."

"Wow, I'd love to come, thanks."

A wintry sun broke through the clouds as Georgia woke. Her auburn hair was tousled on the pillow as she stretched out her body to full length and thought with excitement of the day ahead. She had not told Sophie that she was her second choice for the spa day experience. Katy, her best friend was already booked up.

Desmond, Georgia's husband waved from the doorway.

"Got to dash. Enjoy your day."

Georgia swung her legs out of bed, slipped on her dressing gown and started to pack her bag for the day. She showered and dressed and went to the kitchen to perc the coffee. A quick cuppa when Soph came to collect her and then they would be off for a true girlie pamper day.

The long driveway through the parkland to the splendid building at the end was lined with trees. The girls' mouths dropped open at the grandeur of it all as they carried their bags to the reception desk.

At five-thirty, after a perfect day, they walked to Sophie's car, their feet crunching on the gravel, a breeze blowing gently.

"Will you come in for a drink and share our day out with Des?" Georgia asked as she pulled into the drive. "That's odd, I thought he should be back by now but his car's not here."

Georgia pushed the key into the lock and entered the hallway to put the bunch on the table. Where was the table? She went through to the lounge while Sophie cautiously looked in the kitchen. There was no settee, no furniture in fact.

Sophie handed her a note from the kitchen work top addressed to Georgia.

Our life was not working out. Hope you enjoyed your day.
Katy and I need to be together.
Des.

BEWARE THE GREEKS!
Enid Scoging

John Butler leaned back in his chair, placed his hands behind his head and took a deep breath. Spread in front of him was the list of his tutorial groups. Today would be the last chance he would have to exhort them to work harder at their assignments before the Christmas recess. The first group was due at three thirty p.m. He glanced down at the names. Where did parents dig them up – apart from the *Births* column in the newspapers?

Looking through the window he watched the flurries of snow driven by a high wind, and recalled the early-morning forecast threatening a cold snap. He adjusted his half-rimmed spectacles and awaited the knock on the door and the troop of students clad in obligatory jeans, monstrous sweaters and scruffy trainers.

This afternoon he would try not to look at Mandy too much. The sight of the blonde, nubile student perched on the edge of her chair and leaning eagerly forward caused him to feel a stirring in his loins.

"Are you going, Mandy?"

Barbara stood by the stove in the communal kitchen. Mandy had delegated the task of stirring the scrambled eggs. Looking at her friend's back, Mandy knew she was consumed with curiosity.

'I didn't know you were so friendly with John Butler. In tutorials we've all noticed how he looks at you more than the rest of us. But then, you <u>are</u> brilliant and obviously one of his favourites."

Slightly irritated, Mandy replied: "Of course I'm going. Johnny B is just offering a pre-Christmas drink. His wife will be there and – hopefully – his two sons. Wow! Met them both one weekend at a cricket match."

"You lucky so-and-so," said Barbara, continuing to stir. "Do you like him?"

"Who?"

"Johnny B."

"Well – yes. He's shown a great interest in my work this term <u>and</u> given me lots of help and advice."

"Are you sure it's only your work he's interested in?"

"I'm sure."

"Eggs done. What about the toast?"

Mandy stood at the Butlers' front door, brushing snow from her anorak and stamping her boots free of the clumping white stuff. Lights from the downstairs windows fell in bright splashes across the snow-covered lawn, the crystal flakes glittering and shining. Pressing the bell, she took a deep breath. John Butler, on the other side of the door, also took a deep breath before lifting the latch. And there she stood, her cheeks pink and glowing from the chill wind. He wanted to touch the smoothness of them.

"Come in, Mandy, come in."

She stepped on to the door-mat whilst he took her jacket and she bent to remove her boots.

"Come this way into the sitting-room. Marcia isn't here, I'm afraid. Been held up in London. She'll be a bit late."

The warning bells began to ring in Mandy's head.

"Would you like a drink? Something to warm you?"

"Thank you – perhaps a very small glass of red wine."

John Butler disappeared into the kitchen. Mandy looked around the room, admiring the rows of book-shelves along one wall. The subdued lighting and the crackle of the open fire began to relax her. Coming into the room, her tutor stood in front of her.

"Just look at this." The pieces of a broken corkscrew lay in the palm of his hand.

"Can't open the damned bottle and Peter took our spare back to Edinburgh with him last week." Mandy smiled.

"May I have a coffee instead?" and her host disappeared once more into the kitchen. She looked at the family photographs arranged on a low table. The wedding picture caught her eye. Johnny B had made a very handsome groom. He returned with the coffee.

"Mugs OK?" and she nodded, taking one from the tray. He sat beside her on the large sofa.

"Now, tell me about more about your family. I like to get to know my students' background." He slid an arm along the back of the sofa behind her shoulders, leaning forward and smiling. Mandy put her mug down and reached for her cavernous bag. She rummaged around until she found a brown envelope. She opened it and selected a few pictures. Sitting so close to her, John could smell the freshness of her long blonde hair as it fell across her face.

"I've got some photos of my family. Would you like to see them?" She removed one and handed it to him. "This is my mother. She died when I was born. This is her graduation picture. She was a student here too. I believe she was one of your students. Her name was Maggie Stewart."

John Butler put his coffee mug down with a shaking hand and his thoughts raced back over twenty years. He took the photograph – and recognised the lovely girl he had seduced in a four-poster in a hotel in the heart of rural Oxfordshire.

PITCH PERFECT
Deborah Dunseith

Defender red-carded, referee bombarded
Dissenting, demanding, persisting, relenting
Penalty nominee perspires profusely
Supporters silently, increased expectancy
Managers uptight, flashbulbs ignite
Ferocious velocity, breathtaking accuracy
Goalkeeper spectacularly misjudging trajectory
Stadium erupting, Premiership certainty

THE WEATHER FORECAST
Iris Welford

Rain, sun, drizzle, fog
Thunder, hail, and yellow smog
Snow, ice, frost and haze
Why is the weather such a craze?

AN UPLIFTING EXAMPLE
Sheila Charles

As she drove to meet him, Diana would not be prepared for what was going to happen. Travelling northwards along the deserted hillside road, she would not remember skidding on black ice, or how many times the car rolled over as it left the carriageway and hurtled into the precipice. She would not hear the end of the song she had been singing along to. She would not see the car burst into flames, nor feel the blood streaming down her face, nor smell her burning flesh.

At home, Brogan knew he would be able to shower before Diana was due to arrive. What he didn't know was she wouldn't be turning up. If he had known he wouldn't have needed to go to such lengths – preparing a dinner to remember with an extravagant surprise – to celebrate her return.

He was still in the shower when the phone rang, but knowing she would leave a message explaining she was going to be late, he continued. He unconsciously hummed 'their tune' as he towelled himself dry and then went to check the answer phone. Sure enough, she was going to be late ... again. Well that would give him time to dress and make sure everything was perfect.

After an hour Brogan would feel less confident and more jittery. He would just have one beer to calm the shakes and the old ghosts. He would stay positive and stick to the agreement for another half hour, after which Brogan would open a second bottle, knowing he would somehow never be able to eradicate the past, especially if she didn't stick to her part of the bargain. Brogan had so hoped that this time ... but the memories were getting stronger ... been let down so many times before ... why did he keep falling for such unrealistic promises? He would however keep battling on for another half hour, trying to stick to the Twelve Steps, but after the third bottle he would be less in control and having thrown the meal in the bin he would open the celebratory champagne to drown his sorrows. The time lapse would grow steadily longer and meaner and Brogan's resolve would be thrown to the four winds, together with the carefully laid dining table, the empty champagne bottle and eventually the half-empty whiskey bottle as well.

In the early hours of the next day Brogan would be sprawled over the debris that had once been a romantic candle-lit atmosphere, clutching the large diamond cluster that would have looked so impressive on Diana's finger.

In the meantime the remains of a charred body would be recovered from a burnt-out car found smouldering on a steep embankment of a winding road at eleven twenty-three on a freezing November morning. At the same time, the lifeless body of Dr Brogan McConnacky would be removed from the idyllic cottage where he and his wife had led a turbulent life together for over thirty years.

* * *

The coroner, a long-standing friend, would exclude the blood alcohol levels in his report and the joint funeral would be held in the village church where Diana and Brogan worshipped. The church would be packed to capacity by family, friends and neighbours from far and wide.

Other than knowing that the Doctor 'liked a drink', the finer details of their lives had been well concealed and the service, led by their good friend, Father Dominic,"… was," he would say, "in celebration of a long, happy and successful marriage that has been an uplifting example to us all."

LIKE MOTHER, LIKE DAUGHTER
Rosemary Ford

Most people said that Daisy Carter was a clever girl. Her dad Simon said so, and his mum, Granny Alison, agreed. Daisy's teacher was more inclined to say 'quick-witted', while Granny Andrews thought the same as Daisy's mum, Noeline. They judged Daisy to be shrewd; pleasant, adaptable and knowing how to work things to her own advantage.

A few months ago, just after her bedroom had been decorated in a flamboyant shade of girly pink, Daisy had made a useful discovery. She found that if she lifted the edge of the new carpet by the radiator, she could overhear conversations in the sitting room below. Most of what she heard was dull – talk about work and boring people unknown to Daisy. But sometimes her parents discussed the most fascinating subject of all: Daisy Carter.

"Daisy has got to learn to help around the house more," said Mum. "She's nearly twelve now and she doesn't so much as unload the dishwasher. When I was her age I had to …" Mum's long tale of oppression was interrupted by Dad.

"You're so hard on Daisy. She's still just a kid. And it's not as though you have so much to do. It was your idea to have just one child, so it's no use belly-aching about being overworked."

Dad had raised a difficult subject: that Daisy was an only child. The conversation deteriorated into a tit-for-tat argument, ending in Mum's rapid steps up the stairs and the bang of the bedroom door.

Daisy later used this information to her own advantage by playing off one parent against the other.

"It's so boring for me, Daddy," she would say. "I wish we had a big family like Millie Jones." Or to her mother: "I like it when we go shopping. Just the two of us with no little kids hanging around. It's such fun. Can we go shopping on Saturday? I've seen such a lovely top in *New Look*, and Dad said he would give me the money."

Yes, life was not bad for Daisy.

One night though she overheard a more serious conversation. Dad had been talking about Government cuts so there was no prospect of a useful salary increase for him, and Mum said they were making redundancies in Green's Department Store where she had a part-time job, and that she was a likely candidate.

"Well," Dad said in his deepest, most serious voice, "in the meantime we will all have to CUT DOWN. No new things for the house, no new car, no big holidays, and no new clothes. We've all got plenty of clothes. We've just got to make do."

"Yes," said Mum, safe in the knowledge that she had just placed a large order with her favourite catalogue, "and that goes for Daisy too. She was saying something to me about her school skirt, but she'll just have to make it last."

Upstairs, Daisy took in this information. Actually she didn't want a new skirt at all. What she really wanted was to carry on wearing the old one because it was short. Very short, just like all the older girls wore. So when the subject cropped up she was able to pout and grumble before miraculously agreeing to wear the old one.

"I know we all have to make sacrifices," she said to her proud dad, "so, in the meantime, I'll do my bit by wearing this tatty old skirt for as long as I can."

Dad believed her implicitly, but Mum had her doubts. She understood her Daisy. Like mother, like daughter.

ஒ ஒ

SUNDAY HIGHLIGHT
Enid Scoging

This Sunday was going to be different from the usual routine. As a rule they took the children out somewhere for the day – weather permitting, of course. It didn't need to be an expensive day. A trek through the local woods, coupled with a picnic, was a favourite outing when the sun shone. At other times it was a visit to the swimming pool, plus hamburgers and chips in the adjoining café. Sunday was a day to be with the children, as a family, one unit enjoying one another's company – with any luck!

But this Sunday was going to be different. She leaned against the wash-basin and looked in the bathroom mirror – a bit dark under the eyes, hair wild and unbrushed, skin pale and free of make-up. The years had treated her quite well, she mused, lifting the hair above her ears and searching for the tell-tale signs of greying. The last rinse she'd had at the hairdresser's was holding up quite well.

The sound of yelling voices from the kitchen reached her ears. Squabbling over the plastic toy in the cornflake box yet again. Why couldn't those two learn to share? Well, Steve could sort them out. She needed a few minutes to clean her teeth and brush her hair, tasks which had had to wait because the baby had woken early.

She walked along the landing to the nursery to make sure that little Philip had not been disturbed by the arguing voices from downstairs. She heard the reassuring sound of Steve attempting to solve the dispute. The attempt obviously failed because he claimed the trophy for himself, with the promise of judgement at a later time.

She crept into the little room, the curtains still drawn against the early light. She stood at the cot-side, gazing down at the sleeping form of her third child. The breath came rhythmically, the round face suffused with warm pinkness, and the hands lay clenched on the sides of the head. Beneath the covers the small chest rose and fell and the legs fell apart, held in place by the chunky fit of Pampers. He smelled of baby powder and – after inspection – a very soggy nappy.

Whom did he resemble? Steve? Herself? The two boys downstairs certainly took after their father in looks, with their dark hair and dark eyes. But what about this sleeping angel – all blonde curls and blue eyes. Her own hair was a striking auburn and her brown eyes were set in a pale and freckled face. She leaned over the cot and gently stroked the rounded, downy cheek. The baby breathed a shuddering sigh, smacked his lips and squirmed very slightly. The tiny clenched fists moved and stretched then closed again.

Standing at the foot of the cot, her thoughts returned to the hectic day ahead and its highlight – little Philip's christening. She had to set out the buffet table, and wash and dress the children for the service, which followed the family one. She had to check the guest list, making sure there would be enough china and cutlery to go round. She hoped her mother would remember about the extra milk. She'd forgotten to leave a note for the milkman yesterday.

Her thoughts leaped forward, picturing the assembled guests: grandparents, Godparents, aunts, uncles, cousins – a seemingly endless array of family and friends. Friends! As she went downstairs to begin organising the dining room, she thought of John. Would he be there, in the church, watching the christening of baby Philip? As Steve's best friend of many years his name had been on the guest list, but no reply had come to the invitation. Perhaps it was just as well – but she did wonder. Her throat suddenly tightened as guilty thoughts brought a blush to her cheeks on remembering tall, blonde, blue-eyed John.

☙ ❧

GRANDMA'S RULES
Iris Welford

Becky turned on the bedside light, not sure what had woken her. A low rumble told her that a storm was approaching. She went to the window, opened the curtains and saw a long tongue of forked lightning lick the earth, illuminating the valley in the distance. One, pause, two, pause, three, pause – she counted to seven before the next rumble echoed in her ears. She went to check on Ryan in his bedroom. He was sleeping like the baby he was, oblivious to his mother's fear.

"It's all Grandma's fault," Becky said aloud, mainly to calm herself. "Grandma and her set of rules that would appease Thor and avert disaster."

One by one, Becky went over them in her mind. First you had to open a window on the front of the house, then a window on the back. That meant lightning could get out, if it came indoors. You had to put all knives and scissors in the drawers because they attracted the lightning, and cover the mirrors with cloths. The thought of a cracked mirror was beyond belief. Of course, you had to keep an acorn on a windowsill because that prevented the house being struck in the first place. After all that, you took refuge under the kitchen table or in the cupboard under the stairs.

As Becky was considering these options, the bedside lamp flickered and went out. A loud crack told her the storm was nearer. One and two and three – this time she counted to four which meant the storm was only four miles away. Becky went to the dressing table where she kept a church candle and fumbled in the drawer until she found the matches. Light always made her feel secure. She put on her old jumper and jeans and, with candle in hand, she made her way downstairs to the kitchen where the other candles were kept under the sink. There was no telling how long the power might be off and she had to get the Calor gas cooker working so that she could feed Ryan when he woke.

"Why are men always away when you need them most?" She was near to tears. "Pull yourself together Becky Carson; take control like Grandma."

She placed the candles around the room at strategic points, but was bemused by one candle that flickered continually as if a breeze was wafting around it. Becky realised the draught was coming from the living room but she knew she had not left the French doors or any window open before she went to bed. She shivered. From the cutlery drawer she took her Chinese chopping knife and held it tightly. Gingerly, she inched towards the living room, peering into the corners as she went. The French doors were wide open with the curtains flapping in and out. A loud clap of thunder followed by lightning highlighted a figure about to enter the room. Becky screamed. The noise she made was enveloped in the uproar. Instinctively she hurled the chopper in the direction of the figure that was now leaping towards her. Becky opened her mouth to scream again but fell to the floor.

When she came to, the power had been restored. She was lying on the sofa and the French doors were closed. The room felt normal with no menace, but she could hear her kettle whistling and cupboards being opened. She stood up feeling rather dizzy and padded her way into the kitchen.

"Danny!" She ran to her husband. "What are you doing here? You're not due back till tomorrow."

Danny pulled her close. "I heard the weather warning on the radio and knew you would be jittery. I gave my apologies and left the conference early – but I couldn't phone you from the airport because the phones were out. And when I got here, I couldn't find my door key. I had to use the spare to the French doors."

"You gave me such a fright. I thought we were going to be murdered by some crazed stranger."

"Come with me." Becky followed Danny into the living room. "Murdered? It was me that was nearly murdered!"

Becky looked at the doors. Embedded in the woodwork was her Chinese chopper.

"Thank heavens you haven't got a gun," Danny smiled as he hugged her, "but Grandma would have been proud of you."

Ryan was still asleep when eventually they went to bed.

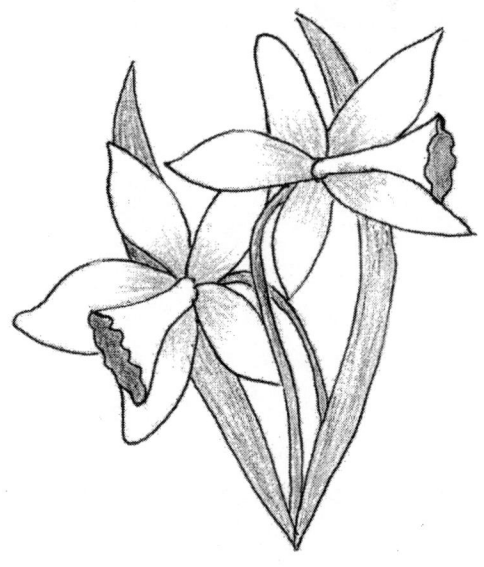

WINTER'S EDGE
Sheila Charles

Caught on Winter's edge,
Silent on the breeze,
Falls a widespread cloth of white.
Eerie death-like hush pervades,
Meantime life endures.

CHRISTMAS TANKA
Rosemary Ford

Twilight magic; candles guttering;
Kindly ladies, icing, buttering.
Stockings hanging, empty, waiting;
Stealthy footsteps upward creaking.
Adults whisp'ring, children listening;
Finally sleeping, fitfully tossing.
Waking: shrieking, squealing, whistling.

HERE I GO AGAIN
Rosemary Davis

Flinging the door open, I shout "Mum, can ...," but before I step over the threshold I hear that song, *Here I go again* ... and I know no one's going to come to tea with me here again.

Mum would be upstairs packing. I turn on my heels and run to the park where I find a large hawthorn bush to crawl under and hope against hope she won't find me.

Ever since I can remember our lives have been a rollercoaster. New place, new school, new friends, and then move on. Never putting roots down for more than six months. I wonder if it was the break-up of the big romance or the unpaid bills this time. I'd heard it all before: "He's so nice, look what he bought me." Some of them had been quite nice, some had actually seemed more interested in me and I'd have to keep out of their way. But in the end they'd take what they could and leave. In the meantime the bills would pile on the table and then Mum would put that record on her little portable player. In the back of my mind I'd been counting: five months, two weeks and three days.

Now it was starting to get dark and I'm hungry but I'm determined not to give in. I hear her voice: "Jenny, Jenny, please come out. You have to be here. I've been to all your friends'. I promise it's going to be different this time."

I bite my lip as I draw my knees up closer to my chest, the damp of the night starting to dampen my resolve. I hear the twigs crack as she searches nearby and as I start to shiver she moves away, still calling.

Then, as if it was a dream, she said: "Jack asked me to marry him. We've got a chance to be happy again."

I'm up and pushing my way out of the bush, not caring about the thorns ripping at my flesh, shouting: "Mum! I'm here," with tears flooding down my face. Now we're in each other's embrace and I'm praying its true and we will have a better future.

WATERSHED
Hazel Gooderson

The old grandfather clock chimed nine.

"Watershed."

He unfurled and stretched his legs.

"Ok, Ethel, safe to go now!"

Any earlier and the young inhabitants took delight in stomping on you, or pulling your legs off.

"Sorry, Stanley, but I'm exhausted; can you bring something tasty back for me and the children?"

Stanley spun out from their residence. It was unfortunate the owners had started to leave bowls of conkers around, restricting his hunting areas.

He worked diligently, accompanied only by the ticking of the clock.

It struck ten. The beautiful silk orb was complete.

Stanley hid and waited.

IT'S A FAKE
Margaret Dutton

"It's a fake."

I spun round to face a small man, rocking on his heels.

"What's a fake?" I asked.

"That rug," and he pointed to a small rug under the beautiful writing table.

I reached for my 'bible'. All information, including dates and provenance, was in the Fact Book under each room steward's chair. I felt unusually nervous. Many visitors to this grand house asked questions; rarely did they give bold facts. And this man had appeared from nowhere. We had been briefed that today's visitors would include a group from a Fine Arts Society and a French school visit. The first would take three hours to walk round the house, the latter five minutes. But this small man didn't seem to belong to either, and he had entered my room from the wrong way.

"Savonnerie rug, c.1643, purchased by the eighth Duke in 1843 as a gift to his mother," I read out from my Fact Book.

"Sure he did. But that rug is a fake." Again, he rocked on his heels. My mother would have called him a spiv with his black hair slicked back, and shiny black jacket. We room stewards were trained to alert our colleagues in case of trouble, but he wasn't threatening. Quite the reverse. He reeled off correctly all the furniture and paintings in Lady Bourne's dressing room, and told me that the French inlaid armoire was signed by Carel, and the Louis XV cupboards were signed by Flechy.

"You're well informed. Have you visited Glasworth House before?"

"Never."

"I'm amazed! How do you know it so intimately?"

"My father was stationed here during the war. He loved antiques. His parents were Armenian and gave him a love of fine things. He used to tell me about this big house and its contents as a bed-time story."

"What did your father do?"

"Dug trenches. He was in the Pioneer Corps. His mob had to prepare this place before it was handed over to the Polish Special Services to train spies to drop behind enemy lines. They also had to pack up all the contents of the house to be sent to Wales for the duration. That's why I know that rug is a fake."

"I'm intrigued ... go on, tell me how you are so sure."

"The real one is on my wall in Cyprus. That one was woven in 1944 by my grandfather, and if you look underneath the large central rose you will see a tiny '44' woven in blue silk. When the house was returned after the war to the family, my dad was one of the removal men."

Against all rules I moved the writing table, turned back the rug, and there *was* a faded '44' under the rose. I stood up shaking at the discovery of ... what? Theft, deception, fraud?

He'd gone of course, and the gentle buzz of the Fine Arts visitors was approaching me. Some of them were very knowledgeable, but none asked about the Savonnerie rug. And until today, I have never told anyone about it either.

THE ROAD TO MATURITY
Rosemary Ford

In the olden days, Breckborough used to boast two grammar schools. By the olden days, I mean the time before everywhere was *comprehensified* and the sexes were mixed together.

One of the town's two grammar schools was of ancient foundation and so, naturally, educated the boys. Just over the road the girls had their own establishment, but not quite so ancient or esteemed. But to the pupils in those days not much thought was given to ancient foundations, but more to the fact that the two sexes were separated by only a busy road and zealous members of staff, so to catch glimpses of boys from 'over the road' was a great excitement to the girls, even if it was only a line of bedraggled fourth-formers being goaded back to lessons from the playing field.

The playing field was large and shared by both schools. Let me make it clear that by 'shared' I do not mean that any fraternisation took place during games lessons, or even that the 'shares' were in any way equal. The boys had a generous two-thirds, set out for rugby or cricket according to season, and an imposing thatched pavilion. The girls had the lower end with a smallish shed for storing hockey sticks and suchlike. So apart from a distant view of the god-like boys being far more interested in doing daring things with rugby balls than noticing Maureen or Sally doing their best not to play hockey, it was more due to the girls' vivid imaginations that any contact was made.

Normally both sides of the road viewed the other when they could and imagined a hundred times more interesting things than actually happened. Such, no doubt, it would have remained had it not been for the weather ... Winters in those days were undoubtedly colder, or so everyone believed. But then again few houses had central heating, so who knows for sure?

But the winter when Sally and Maureen were in the fourth-form was certainly one to remember. October and November were beguilingly mild, although with enough drenching rain to persuade even Miss Dagger, the games mistress, to concede that hockey was 'off'. In December the bitter cold began with treacherous roads and minimal heating, so that the Christmas holidays were a welcome relief. The schools reopened on 8th January. The girls who lived close enough to attend clung to luke-warm radiators and told tales of icicles of amazing length.

The bell for first lesson rang, but no teachers appeared. A young spy in the fifth-form room reported that a staff meeting was going on, and swore that Mr Green, the Head from 'over the road' was there. Later, all was revealed. The boys' school, with its ancient building, had been flooded. All the boys who had managed to arrive were to come over and share lessons with the depleted number of girls.

Bliss! Heaven! Maureen Jones, who had begged her mother to let her stay at home, was so relieved that she had attended, and was even more glad that she had applied even more Amami wave-setting lotion than usual to her mousey hair.

The school sharing went on for nearly three weeks. It felt amazingly lucky to the pupils for a day or two, but then reality set in. They were doing work they had already covered with teachers who did not know them. Worse, the boys, those amazing creatures from over the road, were so ordinary, so silly, so immature, so BORING. When the sun came out at last and things returned to normal even Maureen and Sally were forced to admit that it would be good to go and dribble a hockey ball around the muddy pitch without even looking to see what Adkins or Peterson were doing.

Mind you, if Jack Garland and some of the almost adult young men from the sixth-form were there, they would be worth looking at. As Sally said to Maureen, "Now that we are so much more mature, it's no good pretending to be interested in those silly little boys over the road. But the big ones are well worth a look!"

THINK OF ME
Deborah Dunseith

As the sun goes down and bathes the orchard in
    hues of red and gold
think of me
and the soul that grows no longer old

When the agéd sash windows moan with icy blasts
    and stars are blurred with driving rain
think of me
and the soul that feels no earthly pain

When dewdrops glisten and highlight cobwebs that
    hang across the old shed door
think of me
but learn to love once more

THE IDEAL PARENTS
Sheila Charles

I was fifty before I really understood my parents and, more importantly, myself. The regular chats with Bill had unearthed and explained many things. However, I'm fifty-six now, my position remains unaltered and I have been advised to take further action. But before I do I must set the record straight.

When I was born, my mother was nearly forty, my father was much older and no one knew of my existence. I had no contact with anyone or anything outside our farm. No siblings, no school, nothing. Father had a short temper and a hard fist. Mother had a harsh tongue and an eagle eye. She couldn't bear the sight of me, so I went wherever Father worked, except on Fridays when I was told to keep out of sight. The only affection I got was from the cats in the barn when rat numbers were down and although the river at the end of the bean field was as moody and unfathomable as my parents, it intrigued me and was my only friend. In the winter it raged and grumbled as it stumbled over jagged rocks, warning me to watch my step and bide my time. In the summer, as the water gently rattled over the stony bottom, it sparkled, brightening my gloomy days, just like the cut-glass decanter in our sombre dining room. The ripples reflected dazzling lights in never ending patterns of changing shape and colour, giving me hope that one day things would be different. They reminded me of the diamonds that glittered on Mother's swollen chest, when Father went to market on Fridays and Uncle Arthur called by. Like magnets to my eyes, I was mesmerised by the swell of smooth round flesh as it rose and fell like jelly in a wheelbarrow. As I secretly watched them from the old apple tree overlooking my mother's bedroom, sensations in my loins echoed the illusion of my tongue thrusting a passage through pink marshmallows.

It wasn't until I was older that I understood such images, but it was during my early teens that I began to take some control. The Others were threatening to work with my parents and at night the Naggers taunted me, calling me Custard and Wurzel. I couldn't sleep. I was tormented day and night. The river no longer brought me any comfort. In fact, the Sinners came up from the bottom, enticing me to join them in their murky depths. They told me they were hungry, that I must bring them food. It was then that I knew I must do something.

I had no trouble with Dad; he was after all well into his seventies. I'd fixed the van for him that day and filled the glass decanter. He liked his brandy and always had several 'for the road' before he went to market. I'd checked the rickety bridge over the river. He knew it needed some attention. The verdict, of course was 'Misadventure: Death by drowning while under the influence of alcohol'. But Mother was not so easy, being rather large, tee-total and unable to drive. The Others came up with the answer, and once I had greased the chain-saw and sharpened the blade, I was able to store Mother quite easily in the freezer along with last year's beans.

The following Friday Uncle Arthur called by as usual. Of course he was looking for Mother and he seemed pleased to see her wearing the diamond necklace when I placed his head beside hers in the freezer. With a well-stocked freezer, me and the Sinners were well fed for some time and it was only when the bones were washed downstream that my problems started up again. It was while talking this over with Bill that I discovered Mother and Father were Idealists. They had tried to create an ideal by protecting me from evil and grief. I'm just sorry they weren't Perfectionists because I have had to suffer the indignity of this evil place, and I am still grieving for the river after all these years.

A LATIN ENCOUNTER
Iris Welford

"Ladies and gentlemen," Brian tapped the microphone. "Ladies and gentlemen, your attention please." The chattering stopped as eyes focused on the driver. "We've got four and a half hours here and Alfredo is your guide. He will be showing you the sights. You have time for lunch and we meet again here at three-thirty. Don't be late, because we can't wait. Did you hear that Daphne?" A fit of giggling came from the back. "No, seriously folks, we must join the cruise ship at seven-thirty, so make sure you're back here in good time. Thank you. Alfredo is waiting for you on the car park."

Shirley tapped me on the shoulder. "Would you like to tag along with me and Thelma?"

I turned. "Well, yes I would, so long as I won't be in the way."

Shirley smiled. "Oh good."

Other females often took pity on me, a single traveller; I seemed to bring out their protective instinct, unlike the males who thought that I was a *femme fatale* looking for adventure, but it was reassuring that someone cared.

The Major, as I had nicknamed him, was the first out of the door, followed by his wife, a dowdy little woman who wore brown flat sandals to make sure he looked taller than her. He wore khaki shorts and an olive-green polo shirt and, with his walking stick, still looked the part of an officer on campaign. Out of the window, I could see him directing my fellow travellers towards the guide.

When I reached Shirley and Thelma, Alfredo was raising a green and white striped umbrella in the air.

"What did he say?" I asked Thelma.

"We're going to the church where there's a famous black Madonna, paintings by Tintoretto and a plaque to commemorate the visit of Pope John."

I looked up. I could see the church, complete with its gold embellishment, flying angels and marble statues. Another group of tourists with a red and white striped umbrella were about to enter, whilst a group with a black and white umbrella were descending the stone steps.

"I think I'll give this a miss. I'll go and find the slums and filth."

Shirley looked at me quizzically; she didn't know whether I was joking or not. "Will you be all right on your own, dear?"

"Yes," I said confidently. "I'll see you both later," and I waved as I went in the opposite direction.

The cobbled back streets were dark and narrow. Medieval houses with ancient wooden doors and large wrought-iron handles were mixed together with small shops whose interiors seemed to recede into blackness. I wondered if the sun ever reached these mysterious alleyways and courtyards. People, mostly women dressed in the habitual black, were shopping or standing chatting. Vegetables and bread seemed abundant, as did game like hares and pheasants hanging from butchers' hooks. I continued to wander down the meandering street until I came across a florist shop which had every colour and bloom imaginable. The heady scents wafted around me and I wished that I could buy some of the exotic pink lilies, but it was impractical; they would soon die. Next door to the florist's there was a café with tables and chairs spilling on to the street. It was very busy with office workers, young mothers with pushchairs and teenagers taking their lunch, but I saw a table tucked away in a corner and made for it. After ordering a large Frascati with a chicken salad, I turned my attention to the passers by. I was so absorbed that I neither heard nor saw the man who was standing beside me until I sensed someone close to my face.

"Scusi, signorina, scusi." His citrus aftershave wafted under my nose.

"Oh, I'm sorry," I said startled.

"It's all right; I was asking if I could sit with you, the café is very busy."

"Yes, no, please do." I felt flustered.

He took off his jacket and hung it over the back of the chair. "It's going to be very hot this afternoon I think. Are you visiting the town?" he asked as he sat down.

This time I looked at his face before answering. He was handsome, blue-eyed with a tanned skin, short cropped hair and younger than me. "Yes, my friends are looking at the church but I decided to look at the shops instead."

He chuckled. "Yes, too many churches, too many grand houses, too many sights and not enough relaxation, that is what I found when I was in London."

"You've been to London? Did you enjoy your visit?"

"I studied in London, near Bloomsbury, at Sotheby's Institute. Perhaps you have heard of it? I was studying fine art and business."

"I know the name of Sotheby's, but I live outside of London in a town called Windsor. Perhaps you visited it? It's where the Queen has a castle."

We both laughed. The conversation flowed naturally as we ate and drank and it seemed as if I had known him for years. He told me that his name was Francesco and that he owned his own company advising clients on the best art investments. "But," he said, "money is not everything, I lost my beautiful wife in a car crash three years ago. She went off the road in heavy rain. I still blame myself; I should never have let her go out in such weather."

I felt sorry for him as he related his story. What could I say except, "How awful," and all those platitudes that we use for such occasions? He asked me if I was married and I told him briefly about the divorce, that I did not have to work and had time to please myself.

Francesco had gone to order more wine when I saw the Major and his wife marching down the road. He caught my eye just as Francesco returned and sat down. The Major pointed to his watch in his surly manner whilst giving Francesco a hard stony stare.

"They are friends?" asked Francesco as he looked at the Major.

"No, just fellow passengers."

We carried on talking until I realised that the café had emptied with only a few stragglers left. "What is the time please?"

Rolling back the slightly frayed cuffs of his grey shirt he said, "It's nearly four-thirty. This has been very pleasant, and I hope I have not kept you?"

I chewed my bottom lip, a habit I've had since childhood.

"You are worried?" he asked.

"I have a problem, the coach left nearly an hour ago, and the driver said he could not wait for anyone, as he has to reach the cruise ship by seven-thirty this evening. I cannot phone the office, I don't have the numbers, and I left all the paperwork on the coach. I can get a train …"

"Where are you going then?"

"We're cruising from Venice to Montenegro."

"Very nice, but I have an idea. Let me take you to Venice. In my car it will take about two hours, we will arrive before the coach."

Weighing up the options which were basically non-existent, I said, "Francesco, you're an angel. How kind of you, are you sure?" I squeezed his hand as it lay on the table.

"No problem, I like to help beautiful women." Throwing his jacket over his arm, he said, "Come, we have no time to waste."

I was surprised at the commanding tone of his voice and as we left the café, I imagined Shirley shaking her head saying, "You will be careful dear?" But then I dismissed the thought and eagerly followed Francesco onto the bustling street.

FOG
Enid Scoging

The greyness swirled
And twisted voluptuously,
Weaving its way between
Misshapen ghostly forms.
The fog concealed shapes
And contorted figures.
It hid trees and buildings,
Fences and people,
Gluing them in its
All-enveloping shroud.
Sounds were muted
And footsteps muffled.
Voices drifted
Through leaden streets,
And orange lights failed
To guide the wary walker
As their rays were caught
In coils of drifting grey.

MOVING THE SUMMERHOUSE
Hazel Gooderson

The time had come to get a bigger summerhouse.

Sunday dawned warm and sunny. The Cartwright family of Number Five, Bluebell Road all mucked in together to empty out its contents.

The young twins joked about their paintings from nursery days pinned around the wooden walls and then screwed them up for the dustbin. Dad's etchings, stored behind the old battered sofa, were quickly removed from prying eyes. Mum's desk, piled high with half-finished stories, pen-pots and art materials, was cleared and then lifted into the waiting tent, specially erected for the couple of days between demolition and the laying of the new base in readiness for the larger model.

* * *

"Goodbye Tiddles – look after the house for me, I'll bring you back a nice bit of fish for your lunch."

Maureen shut the front door of her cottage, Number Five, Buttercup Lane.

Tiddles, the large four-year-old tortoiseshell cat, sat on the windowsill and licked her paw. "I'm far too busy to stay awake and be a guard cat."

Justin and Jake entered the garden through the back gate and, slowly and methodically, worked for twenty minutes before resting for a flask of tea and cake.

"You know Justin, I could write a book about the things people keep in their outhouses, particularly when this one was supposed to be empty."

Refreshed from his tea-break, Justin climbed onto the roof and pulled out the nails. Their job was to remove the wooden structure, before colleagues arrived to lay a larger base for the new construction. Within two hours, the old summerhouse had been dismantled, loaded onto the vehicle, and *The Right Company*, noted for their excellent workmanship, swept the old base clean.

At half past twelve, Maureen Carthouse opened her front door. "Hello Tiddles, I'm home. Let's get the kettle on."

As she turned the cold tap on, she stared out the window at her garden and suddenly shouted: "Where's my … summerhouse gone?!"

MEANTIME
Margaret Dutton

Popeye hated going to his Nan's. She was mean and nasty; her pinched mouth never smiled or said a kind word. His other grandmother was lovely, but after the divorce he didn't see her again. She sent exciting birthday and Christmas presents, and Mum made him write back immediately to say thanks. But Nan would scoff at the gifts; he saw her once try to break an Airfix model that Granny had sent. Nan lived in Greenwich, and he thought Greenwich Mean Time was named after her.

When he stayed at Nan's, she made him go to bed in the afternoon. He wasn't tired or ill nor a baby; it was a way of getting rid of him for a few hours. Lying on the lumpy bed staring at pictureless walls, the sun filtering through thin plain curtains, his imagination had him on the deck of HMS Hood, alongside his Grandpa, bravely manning the guns before she went down in 1941, taking Grandpa and fourteen hundred other souls.

Downstairs in the dreary cabbage-reeking hall, the ticking Westminster clock marked the hours and minutes of utterly boring tedium. Tick, tock, tick, tock, he counted to the chimes. He learnt to tell the time in half-hour segments whilst listening to the laughing kids outside kicking balls against Nan's house, and calling her 'Rat-bag'. He would peep through the curtains and giggle at their cheek. That's how he got his nickname – they knew he was there, but only seeing one of his eyes, they called out 'Popeye' and the name stuck.

He moved to senior school, but Mum was busier than ever, so trips to Greenwich were more frequent. He wasn't put to bed, but he wasn't made welcome either. No TV, no radio, and harder still, no books. Homework was his escape and the teachers were impressed, especially with his technical skills. Nan's neighbours took pity on him – a place for Popeye would be laid at many a table. He learnt that his Grandpa was highly respected, and that he was a 'chip off the old block'.

Sadly, his mother was also a 'chip off the old block'. She too died as a result of enemy action; blown to pieces by an IRA bomb on her way to work at the Old Bailey. Popeye's world collapsed. The horror of losing his mum was intensified by the thought of permanently living with Nan.

The kindness of strangers and friends took over. A phone call here, a meeting there, and soon Popeye was at the Royal Naval College at Dartmouth, training to be a gunnery officer. He thrived, was popular, and loved all the girls who loved a sailor; he was never going to settle for a mean, nasty one. He dutifully took a few back to Greenwich to visit Nan, but the cold reception they received made it less and less frequent.

His first commission was HMS Tireless, one of the Royal Navy's Trafalgar-class submarines. He was responsible for the newly-installed nuclear warheads. His star was rising, his superiors confident in his diligence and duty. Popeye the sailorman found his Olive, a lovely Devon girl, Tessa, who made him laugh, and without a mean bone in her delightfully sexy body. His uniform brushed by her to perfection, he proudly strode up the gangplank and saluted the quarterdeck of his first ship. After two months, he and a skeleton crew took the submarine out for sea trials. All went well; a few niggles, mainly from the CPO cook, but everything was shipshape, and he relaxed and wrote to Tessa.

His Artificer Chief Petty Officer called him and requested he come immediately.

"There's a problem with the timing in number three torpedo, Sir. It's very slightly retarded, and that puts the firing time out too. Might be nothing, thought you should check."

Popeye moved swiftly through the tidy narrow corridors of the submarine. His CPO, a thoughtful man with years of gunnery experience, was staring at the control panel, and writing figures on the log sheet.

"I've re-checked our timing, even used Greenwich Meantime pips, but there is a problem, and it's getting worse, Sir. Listen to that ticking, it's out of kilter: tick, tick, tickety, then pause, then tick, tick."

Popeye and his Chief knew there was an increasing risk a timer was galloping away, and could accidentally set off a torpedo.

"Evacuate the ship," he ordered. "I'll check the ruddy timer Chief … and no arguments," he said to head off the older man's protests.

The submarine surfaced, the crew scrambled into inflatable lifeboats, and had just moved safely away when HMS Tireless exploded with a massive plume of flames, water, and metal.

Popeye was awarded the George Cross; at his memorial service only one chair was empty …

RED SEA
Rosemary Davis

Red sea of sunshine glowing all around.
Black clouds tumbling down.
Grey mist blanketing all the sound.
Snow white creating mound after mound.

❧ ☙

THE WEATHERMAN
Iris Welford

There's snow outside my mother said
I pulled the duvet round my head
I was like toast in my snug little bed
Then the weatherman on TV said
More heavy snow is on its way
There may be drifts as it will lay
Stay indoors for the rest of the day
Unless of course you have a sleigh
I curled my toes in sheer delight
Closed my eyes as tight as tight
Mother knew the man was right
In bed I'd stay all day and night

❧ ☙

THE SHE-WOLF – A CHRISTMAS FAIRY TALE
Sheila Charles

His nose was as red as the legendary reindeer's as he strode through the snow towards the distant light. Max blew on his hands and wished that he had taken up his father's offer of a lift. The wind's icy edge penetrated through his coat and he pulled the red hood closer round his neck. He struggled to keep his balance; the snow had drifted, forming miniature mountains and sharp shadows. It was hard going.

Max was on his way to his grandmother's, delivering her Christmas present and some groceries. He'd set off later than usual because his friends had bet him he wouldn't dare walk through the woods at night. He'd show them he wasn't afraid of the She-wolf. Once in the wood, sheltered from the icy blast, his backpack was weighing heavily. It was then Max remembered Gran's present weighed a ton! He rummaged roughly through the back pack, ripping the Christmas paper off it. He retied the ribbon round the neck of the bottle, after taking a large swig or two, thinking, "Gran's half blind so she won't notice."

Max felt warmer now and began to clamber through the snow again when he heard footsteps behind him. He turned and saw a pair of iridescent green eyes staring at him. The hairs on the back of his neck felt all prickly and a wave of fear trickled down the full length of his spine. Terrified, Max ran as fast as he could, stumbling and slipping, but he didn't stop until he reached his gran's little cottage, relieved to have arrived in one piece. Pale but no longer cold, breathless and frightened, he looked behind him and again he saw that iridescent green. He opened the door, shutting it with a bang, calling out, "Hello Gran. It's me."

"You're late. I thought you'd forgotten me," Gran replied. "I'm down in the cellar, won't be a tick. Start putting the stuff away, there's a dear."

Max had almost emptied his backpack when there was a knock at the door. Remembering that he hadn't locked it, Max felt the hairs rise on the back of his neck for the second time that evening. He rushed to slide the bolts across, noticing a strange green glow seeping through the gaps. With trembling hands he opened the spy-hole. He was blinded by the menacing iridescent green.

"Who is it, Max?" His gran shouted up from the cellar.
"N … n … no one, Gran, n … nothing," Max lied, stepping back from the door.

"I'm not deaf, Max! Who is it? I'm expecting my neighbour."

Max faltered, unsure what to do. He took another look through the spy-hole and through the green glow a voice said, "Hurry up will you Edie, this thing is heavy."

By the time Max had slid the bolt across to open the front door, Gran was standing next to him.

"Whatever's the matter, Max? You're shaking like a jelly! Did you meet the She-wolf in the forest?" she joked. "C'mon, let's get Arthur in out of the cold, before he catches his death. Look he's brought my Christmas tree round. Ooh, green lights and all!"

Max sighed with relief. "Oh, that must have been you in the forest. I know the She-wolf is a legend but those green lights did have me wondering." They all laughed about Max's sighting of the green-eyed She-wolf over a few drinks and a piece of Gran's melt-in-your-mouth lemon cake.

"I'd better be going before I get snowed in," Max said, hearing the wind howl and seeing thick snow flurries hurtling past the window.

"You take care, Max, its pretty wild out there, and watch out for those green eyes," Gran joked. "Oh, and thanks for the present," Gran called out as Max walked off into the night, with a warm glow inside his chest.

He wasn't sure whether it was the strong wind, the drifts or the drink that made it so difficult to stay upright! Half way home, he stumbled and fell for the umpteenth time, hitting his head on the jagged rock that is said by legend to be the resting place of the Great Ulfred. Now some say that Max dreamt what happened next but some folk believe it to be true.

The much-feared She-wolf, Fridolf, visited the spot where the Great Ulfred was shot and buried over one thousand years ago. The She-wolf returns every year on the anniversary of his death. On this same night, Fridolf is pleased to find Max lying there and paws his shoulder.

"Max, wake up, come with me." The dazed Max walks with Fridolf towards a green glow in the distance. A throng of people and creatures are making merry: dancing, eating and drinking, singing and laughing. When Fridolf and Max appear, a hush descends and hundreds of iridescent green eyes stare upwards in wonder at the earthling and the She-wolf.

Fridolf speaks, the crowds cheer and two turtle doves swoop down carrying a long golden robe that they drape around Max and the She-wolf. As they gaze into one another's eyes, the She-wolf is transformed. Shrivelled, leathery skin replaces her fur-covered face, her features become more human and Max recognises the archetypal wise woman. But the wrinkles begin to vanish and curls caress the cheeks of a young maiden. The crowd applauds as a partridge, with a glistening white collar, glides down from a pear tree. He slides his beak through five gold rings nestling on a velvet cushion upheld on a fountain of glittering dust. The partridge tosses the rings into the air. As they cascade in serpent-like twists, they unite to form a single band of gold that comes to rest on the marriage finger of Max's left hand. The couple kiss and the crowd's jubilant applause echoes round the valley.

Shortly afterwards Max awoke, lying in his bed, recalling the 'vivid dream', but was alarmed to feel the gold ring on his finger and see the golden cloak at the foot of the bed. He tried it on, pulling the hood over his head and Fridolf appeared before him.

"Surely I must still be dreaming."

"Not so, dear Max. By wearing the cloak and the five gold rings, the spell on me has been broken, and I can take my rightful place as the Queen of the Forests. You can keep the ring but I need the golden cape to protect me from my wicked step-father, and finally, before I leave, I can grant you one wish.

Max knew that his friends would never believe this story and he wasn't really sure whether he did, except he has the broad gold band, owns a shiny new golden Porsche and lives in a mansion with his gran and Arthur in a place where there are no iridescent green-eyed creatures.

ಶ ಶ

THE SAMOVAR
Margaret Dutton

Both were foreign, exotic and shiny. One was a strange looking metal pot perched on a pedestal in the window. The other was a woman whose bust and bottom were struggling to keep within her green silk dress. As we stood outside the newly opened café, the door burst open and she insistently invited us in.

"Velcome to 'The Samovar', named after the object of your desire in my vindow! I'm Bekka," she said grandly. "Please take a seat and I vill bring some tea, and my special orange soaked rhum-baba."

She sashayed away and Ken and I giggled at the grand gestures, and the larger bottom. "It's been done up very nicely," smiled Ken, looking at the freshly painted walls, and fingering the smart covered tables.

Bekka brought the tea, and sat down opposite us. She leaned towards Ken, and sighed huskily. "Such lovely eyes – I love blue eyes. Lucky you," and she winked at me. Over delicious cake and tea, we learnt she'd opened the café 'on a ving and a prayer' and wanted as many recommendations as we could make. "All I have is my Polish grandmother's samovar and a little money, so this must succeed! Do you live locally?"

We did, and Ken worked locally too, which excited her. "You must bring your colleagues here," she begged.

It was the early sixties, Beatles music was beating, and Bekka was years ahead of her time as far as publicity was concerned. No event was missed to make a grande-dame entrance. Soon the whole town was talking about 'The Samovar' and it opened in the evenings for 'intimate suppers'. Rumours started that the intimate part of the supper was indeed very intimate, with curtained-off rooms and large sofas. Taxis were asked to take customers to that 'silver tea-urn place', and our sedate High Street gained some notoriety.

Gossip and envy grew apace. Bekka employed young girls as waitresses, but that was the polite description. Within a year she expanded into the next door premises, but still held coffee mornings for charity and was especially generous to the Soldiers Sailors Airmen and Families Association. Men who would never ever attend coffee mornings flocked to 'The Samovar' to be held in her thrall – and bosom – and promised to return.

Needless to say, the women of our town became uneasy. "Pompey's the place for knocking shops ... not here," said my outspoken neighbour. "And I think you should have a word with your Ken. Bill saw him leaving 'The Samovar' last week, a bit drunk, according to Bill."

Angrily I tackled Ken that night when he came home very late.

"Oh, bloody hell, Trish, if you only knew!"

"Try me," I snarled through gritted teeth.

"Well – you know I can't tell you everything about work; and I doubt if you'll believe me if I say part of my job at the moment is keeping an eye on 'The Samovar'," and he looked so forlorn, and drunk, that I didn't know whether to hug him or hit him.

Ken was technical director of a large telecommunications firm, travelled all over the world, and never once had I doubted him. But now I felt unsure.

"That bloody Bekka fancied you the moment she saw you – with her husky breath and heaving breasts ... men are so weak when it's offered to them on a plate. Is that what this is about?" I cried.

"Give me some credit, Trish. I've had gorgeous girls offered to me from Rome to Rio; far, far better than big bum Bekka, and I know the score. They're bait, and we know it. Bekka's not what she seems, believe me!"

"Well you're taking a mighty long time finding out. Next you'll be saying she's a Russian spy ..."

"No ... but she's probably married to one! She's not Polish, her husband is a Russian Naval Commander, who suddenly seems to have left this mortal coil. Russia wants him, and so do we. We're now aware why Bekka opened the café in this town – conveniently between Portsmouth Naval Base and our new telecommunications systems factory. We're being 'entertained' by Bekka in the hopes something will be exposed. But what, we don't yet know."

I laughed at this. "Well that takes the biscuit for an excuse! The Beatles' *Hard Day's Night* seems to have been written for you!"

We went to bed, lovingly made up, and I believed him ...

A few months later the High Street was closed off by the police and military; Bekka had disappeared, never to be found, the café searched, 'waitresses' interviewed, but nothing was ever discovered. A nine-day wonder, the town remembered those days, the world soon forgot.

* * *

That was then, and decades rushed past. Ken retired, and took up sailing, I started painting and writing, and life jogged along quietly. The dreaded decision to 'downsize' lurked. "*To move or not to move*, that is the question," Ken kept muttering, so we had a big clear out in preparation. The loft was first. Dust, detritus, and so many memories came tumbling down from that roof space. We laughed, cried, and cuddled at the sight of long forgotten items. Children's toys, camping equipment, 'just in case' pieces were rediscovered, and brutally discarded. A huge box came through the loft hatch. It was far too large and heavy for me to hold standing on the steps, and it crashed down.

"Are you OK?" shouted Ken, peering down on me, covered in dust and cobwebs.

"Yes, I'm fine, but let's call it a day, and see what this box contains," I said wearily.

Over tea and cake, we renewed our acquaintance with the samovar. I was stunned. Ken looked uncomfortable, and wriggled on his chair.

"I'd forgotten about that," he said sheepishly. "Years later when all that café fuss died down, the police came to my office and said they were closing the case, and had found an instruction that I should be given the samovar. They checked everything out and it was pukka."

"Whose instruction?" I asked, already guessing the answer.

"Bekka's. And I knew that would make waves – unjustly – between you and me."

"So you hid it in the loft! Why you?"

Even more sheepishly he said, "She wrote a letter saying she had taken a shine to me but that I was the most honourable of men, and deserved it."

"Bloody big-bum Bekka! She nearly wrecked us, but I am not going to let her do that again. Get rid of it. Sell it."

"I must confess I'd wanted to do that when it landed on my desk," said Ken, rubbing his chin. "I'll contact Jim at the auction rooms, to see if he thinks it's worth a punt."

Worth a punt was an understatement. It goes on sale at Sotheby's today. The Russian Art market has exploded, the auctioneers said huge interest had been expressed for the rare silver gilt 1840 samovar, which experts indicated had belonged to the last Tzarina, Alexandra of Russia.

Take That's *Shine* fizzes out from our car radio as we make our way to the auction in London. Ken smiles, looks at me and says, "I'll get a new boat, Trish, a twin-engined job, not too large, and how about we call her *Shiny Samovar*?"

☙ ❧

HIS SAINTED MOTHER
Rosemary Ford

Today was to be a very special day for the young couple. Kevin was going to move in with Kayleigh in their own little flat, where Kayleigh had already lived for six months, so she had it nice and homely. Kevin had wanted to move in sooner but he had to think about his poor old mum. It was four years now since she had been widowed, but she still depended on her only son. Kayleigh didn't like to complain. After all, it showed what a nice considerate boy he was. But now, at last, the glorious day had arrived. Most of Kevin's things were already there, and tonight, Valentine's night, was to be the beginning of their happy life together.

Kayleigh had rung into work that morning to say she had an upset stomach so that she had all day to prepare the special meal. She had bought a selection of pricey magazines and was bemused by all the ideas, but finally made her selection and went shopping. She also bought a long strip of card and some felt-tips. On the card she wrote in large letters: 'KAYLEIGH AND KEVIN, THEIR OWN SPECIAL HEAVEN'. This she propped up over the bed in their little bedroom.

Now she turned her attention to the all-important love food. She was going to do a very elaborate starter involving goat's cheese, apricot salad and figs, but then it occurred to her that Kevin didn't like anything that he called 'mixed-up food'. Anyway, it was very difficult, so she abandoned it.

The main course was all-important. One of the magazines had described fish as 'love food', so she bought some sea bass. It was a bit slippery and scaly and ugly but it certainly had a real fishy smell and she felt sure it would be a special treat. It was certainly expensive enough. Next she fiddled and struggled with the dessert, which was supposed to be heart-shaped. It looked a bit of a mess, but if the worst came to the worst they could always have ice-cream.

Kevin should be there at any moment, hopefully bearing a large bunch of red roses and an amorous expression. Kayleigh had a quick wash and changed into the little mauve number that Kevin liked. She had just smeared on some make-up and a generous spray of perfume when she heard the sound of the key in the lock; the sound she had been waiting for. Then she heard the voice – the voice of his sainted mother.

"Cor blimey, Kev, what's that dreadful stink? Don't that dumb girl of yours know the only fish you can eat comes shaped like fingers?"

Kayleigh was beyond tears. She just managed to pull down the redundant banner before she thrust the covers over her head without bothering to take off the mauve dress. But she had to go and scrub and scrub her hands to try to dispel the overwhelming fish smell ...

A SOCIAL GATHERING
Enid Scoging

"Lady Hillingdon? It is you. How good to see you here."

Lady Hillingdon looked up at the new arrival, noting the startling colour of the speaker's elegant dress.

"I'm so sorry but I do not think …"

"Forgive me. It is so many years now. Allow me to introduce myself – I'm Marie, Duchesse de Buccleugh."

Lady Hillingdon shook her head, the golden tresses catching the auditorium lights. "You must forgive *me*. I did not recognise you immediately. Memory plays such tricks."

Lady Hillingdon stood to face the Duchesse who leaned forward, placed a Gallic kiss on each of her cheeks and then looked around.

"I see we are to share a box here in the Norwich Theatre Royal. Such a beautiful building. It has the re-decorations, non?"

"Yes," replied Lady Hillingdon, "and at great expense. But come, please be seated."

The Duchesse sank gracefully on to a chair, carefully arranging her full-skirted, magenta-pink gown over her knees. Lady Hillingdon returned to her place and rearranged her apricot and yellow gown equally carefully and thinking: *Pity our two dresses clash so much.*

"Now my dear Lady Hillingdon, who is here tonight? I think I see many familiar faces but the names I do not remember."

Lady Hillingdon leaned forward, pointing discreetly: "There's Albéric Barbier. A dear soul. Delightfully muddled at times. Remember him? Always wears a creamy-white dress-shirt. His shoes are so highly polished, one can see one's face in them."

The Duchesse turned her head. "I believe that is – ah yes – Roger Lamelin, is it not? Always wears a maroon-fringed white shirt – and he looks quite, er, délicat, non?"

"Yes," confided her companion. "He needs extra care these days. But he manages to survive. Just look over there – you must remember Ena Harkness: a dedicated social climber. Always wears dark red velvet and a heavy perfume. She's a listener – see how her head is bent forward? Developed a weak neck from leaning over so much, <u>and</u> she's very free with her favours!" sniffed Lady Hillingdon.

The Duchesse raised her eyebrows before remarking, "I think I recognise Mrs Colville in that box. I have met her many times. A fascinating lady, but such a – busy frock! Too many white dots. And isn't that her daughter Chloris beside her? A lovely dress. That flesh colour suits her well. So petite, so belle."

"Ah, here comes the guest of honour," whispered Lady Hillingdon. "We are here to celebrate his birthday, you know."

They both turned to watch as The Bishop swept into the empty box next to theirs, his robes of magenta, cerise and purple quite overshadowing the white gown of Mrs Herbert Stevens, his wife.

Behind her hand, Lady Hillingdon said to the Duchesse, "She's such a wonderful support to The Bishop. Her stamina is absolutely remarkable."

The audience rose to its feet, the rustling of colourful attire mingling with polite applause.

"I do hope The Bishop will enjoy the performance," remarked Lady Hillingdon. "He chose the programme <u>and</u> requested all the wonderful flower arrangements. 'Nothing but roses,' he insisted." Lady Hillingdon opened her programme. "Do you know this opera?" she asked the Duchesse, "Der Rosenkavalier?"

"Mais oui. Naturellement!"

* * *

DRAMATIS PERSONAE

LADY HILLINGDON: An outstanding rose, combining shapely apricot-yellow flowers with healthy plum-coloured shoots and grey-green leaves. A climber.

DUCHESSE DE BUCCLEUGH: Almost thornless. The large, fully double flowers are flat, quartered and of a rich magenta pink. Fragrant.

NORWICH THEATRE ROYAL: Plumpish buds open up to double pillar-box red flowers. They are borne in small erect clusters and exude a soft perfume. Foliage when young is olive-green tinged with copper and matures to a rich mid-green.

ALBERIC BARBIER: A vigorous rose, creamy-white flushed yellow. Delightfully muddled when open. Excellent glossy foliage. Good variety.

ROGER LAMELIN: Maroon-fringed white double. Needs extra care.

ENA HARKNESS: Still one of the best fragrant reds but has a weak neck. Strongly scented. Very free-flowering.

MRS COLVILLE: A fascinating little shrub with single purple-crimson blooms with a white eye.

CHLORIS: Full, small flesh-coloured flowers on a compact erect bush.

THE BISHOP: Rosette-shaped flowers, an unusual mixture of magenta, cerise and purple. Fragrant, and flowers early. Upright habit.

MRS HERBERT STEVENS: A lovely white variety to be found in many gardens because of its stamina. Fragrant and vigorous.

Names and descriptions of roses by kind permission of Peter Beales, of Peter Beales Roses, Attleborough, Norfolk.

WATERSHED?
Deborah Dunseith

Thongs, suspenders, erotic dancing
"What *is* the time?" I find myself asking
It can't yet be the watershed
My youngest two are no near bed

Check programme listings, its seven forty-five
The living room has come alive
"Phwoar she's sexy," our pre-teen drools
My husband looks up from checking his pools

Thrusting, flirting, high heels go prancing
I only switched on for 'Strictly Come Dancing'
My young son shrieks, "She's got a whip!"
A shimmy of cleavage and a grind of the hip

Whilst I grapple with remote controls
I glance down at my belly rolls
And wish that I looked quite that cute
Cavorting in my birthday suit

THE LEOPARD-SKIN BIRD
Hazel Gooderson

Justin Lennox rubbed the lens of his binoculars, and with the same crisp white handkerchief, laundered by his mother, mopped his brow.

He had a 'six-pack' toned body and was a shift worker, which explained how he was able to be bird-watching at twelve noon on a Monday. His pale green eyes had a hint of sadness. It was only when his close mate, Tony from Blue Watch, invited him out on the fens to help him over his recent grief that Justin had reluctantly agreed, and started this new hobby. The tall, remarkably good-looking man in his late twenties was wearing blue jeans and a faded T-shirt stretched across his chest.

Meanwhile, Annabel Lacey stepped out onto the patio of her new home. She undid the buttons of her pink and white striped blouse, revealing two large and rounded breasts just captured in a leopard-skin patterned bikini top. Unzipping her shorts and stepping out of them, she neatly folded the clothing and placed it into her canvas bag. Sitting on the edge of the sun-lounger, she removed the bottle of sun factor fifteen and unscrewed the cap. She squeezed a quantity onto her palm and tenderly caressed her right leg, running her hand down to her 'luscious cherry' painted toenails and back up. On her other leg, she paused to study the latest blemish. A bruise the size of a saucer was yellowing on her upper thigh.

"That blessed trolley, when will I ever learn?"

She followed the same process for her arms, stroked her stomach in gentle circular movements and finished with her pretty face. She fixed the ear pieces of her MP3 player and settled back to absorb the vitamin D into her aching body and forget the night at work.

It was the morning after and, soon, the soft-playing music had lulled her to sleep. A restless sleep, burdened with frightening images.

"Justin, I've brought you a cuppa love. I was making one for your dad before I go to the shops. Have you seen anything new today?"

"No Mum, it's not the best time of day really. These binoculars are brilliant though, much stronger than Dad's old ones. Thanks, Mum."

"Well you deserved them, son."

"Thanks for the tea, Mum," Justin called to the retreating woman. He also meant to ask his mum if she had new neighbours.

The powerful binoculars had followed a chaffinch gathering nesting material over the garden wall into old Mr Carpenter's garden, where Justin had found a stretched-out, skimpily-clad female of the Caucasian species. His eyes travelled the length of her body, admiring the bronzed flesh. His own body started to awake after weeks of slumber. He needed to introduce himself, but how? A cup of sugar from his mother's larder was not appropriate.

Annabel awoke to the sun glittering on glass. It was coming from the upstairs window of next door. She remained still and tried to squint through half-open, thick-lashed eyes to see what was causing the glint.

Justin realised he had been rumbled. He had to think quickly. He leaned out of the bedroom window.

"Er ... hi, fancy a drink?"

༄ ༅

LOVE IN THE PARK
Iris Welford

Emily took another bite of her cheese sandwich. The park was lovely at this time of the year and her bench was always empty. Though nobody spoke to her, Emily didn't mind; at least she was out of her dreary house.

On the seat opposite a young woman waited for the middle-aged man who Emily felt in her bones was definitely not her father. She had watched them for several weeks and was convinced the man was the young woman's lover. She saw the way he devoured the girl with his eyes. The girl responded with adoring glances and soft touches to his arm. They always spoke in whispers but sometimes Emily caught the odd sentence. "Have you told her yet?" was a sentence the young woman had uttered more than once. But Emily never heard what he replied because he always bowed his head and looked at his knees when he was asked that question. "A cheat if ever there was one," she decided.

Today the young woman seemed more agitated than usual and *lover boy*, as Emily called him, was late. Emily retrieved her battered Thermos flask from her carrier bag and began to slowly pour its steamy liquid into the plastic cup. The young woman put her mobile phone to her ear. Emily strained to hear what the woman said.

"Tom, it's me. Wondered if you've been delayed? Really important I see you, give me a ring. Michelle."

Emily was intrigued. She decided that *lover boy* Tom had ditched poor Michelle because his wife had found out about their affair; that's what usually happened when middle-aged men didn't want to pay for a divorce.

Emily caught Michelle's eye. "Would you like a cup of coffee, dear?" she asked.

Michelle smiled politely. "No thank you, but it's kind of you to ask."

"I'm Emily. I've seen you once or twice when I've been in the park. Do you usually come at lunchtimes?"

Michelle came and sat beside her. "Yes, I meet my friend, but he's late today. I don't know what could have happened to him."

Emily saw Michelle's eyes start to fill and a lone tear dashed down her cheek. "I expect he's been delayed in the office or something, dear, you know what these men are like. Don't worry he'll be here in a jiffy." She hoped she sounded reassuring.

The young woman swept her hair back from her face and took a deep breath. "He does have an important job in the council offices; he often has to work late. We don't get as much time together as we used to."

"He's got another woman," Emily thought but didn't say. "Have you got a nice job, dear?"

"Yes, I'm a teaching assistant at Blackfriars. I love being with children. They're full of fun."

"Have you and your friend been going out long?" asked Emily.

"Nearly two years," she murmured. Michelle looked at her watch. "I really must go, I've got to be at work by one fifteen." She stood up. "If my friend comes and looks for me, can you tell him that I've gone to school?"

"Yes, of course, dear."

"Thank you so much, I hope to see you again." Michelle started to jog down the path towards the gates.

Half and hour later having finished her picnic, Emily decided to make a move. Out of nowhere *lover boy* appeared and Emily called to him. "Excuse me, the young woman asked me to give you a message."

Tom turned. "You've seen Michelle?"

"How very abrupt. Pompous ass," thought Emily. "Yes, she waited and she phoned you."

"I left my mobile at home," he said. "What is the message?"

Again Emily bristled at his imperious manner. "Typical council stuffed shirt," she thought. "I definitely don't like him."

"She said she was going …" Emily paused and changed her mind. "She said she wouldn't be coming to the park again because her hours at work had been changed and she doesn't want to lose her job by being difficult."

Tom looked astounded and said, "I can't believe she said that."

Emily shrugged her shoulders and stepped nearer to him. "I reckon she's on to you, I reckon she knows what you're up to with your late nights and never enough time." She looked him squarely in the eye. "She's found you out. Good job."

Emily clasped her Tesco bag and hurried down the path, congratulating herself. "No more lunchtime lovey-dovey for him, at least not with that nice young girl," she muttered. "I do enjoy helping young gullible girls and Michelle was my second one this month. I think I'll move to the other side of the park tomorrow and see what goes on over there," as she began to hum *Love is in the Air*.

ROYAL WEDDING
Margaret Dutton

In perfumed lilac-time,
a prince and maid
stand tall.
The public frenzy calms,
and hatted heads are still,
to hear the stone-strong vows:
"I will."
All honest hearts would pray
that this young couple will,
one far-off day,
remember lilac-time …
and smile.

THE OUTING
Enid Scoging

"Are you ready then?"

Fred clenched his teeth – his new set. They hurt a bit and that's why he was feeling a bit irritable. *Of course I'm bloody ready. Can't you see?* But he didn't say it out loud. Young Molly was a good lass. He relied on her to take him whenever he needed to be taken somewhere.

He'd been ready since early morning, dressed in his warm zip-up cardigan and padded anorak. Ready with his hospital-issue walking stick and his hospital-issue boots with their Velcro straps.

"Have you got everything?" Her brown eyes smiled as she touched his shoulder. He liked that. Made him feel special instead of the old crock he really was. Hospital today, check-up at the clinic, the full works. He even liked that – being made a fuss of by, not one, not two, but maybe even three different people with any luck. Molly called it his MOT.

And it was a day out – away from his saggy old chair, the ticking clock and the smell of cabbage from the dining room. He took Molly's arm. She always offered an arm. He liked that. Together they walked along the front path to the waiting car – a people-carrier it was called. He found that out from Molly. The usual gang of fellow decrepits was already seated. Mrs Foster was there, banging on the window and waving. And he liked that, too. Tom the driver was standing by the door, his usual bright and chatty self.

The waiting area in the Clinic for the Elderly was crowded. Molly checked him in at reception, found him a seat and patted him on the shoulder as she left to take Mrs Foster to a different department.

Fred sat quietly, stick held between his feet. Idly, he twiddled it around. He strained to hear his name called. The constant comings and goings made that difficult. He closed his eyes – and waited.

With a sudden jerk, he came to. He heard the shouting, the cursing, the pounding of feet. Eyes, heads and bodies turned in the direction of the uproar. The dishevelled figure, with flailing arms and lashing feet, was crashing its way along the corridor with the burly porters closing in on him. Patients and staff pressed themselves against the walls to avoid any contact.

Fred felt a surge of adrenalin. He rose to his feet. Facing the oncoming assault, he pushed his sturdy hospital-issue walking stick forward at a sharp angle – and caught the frantic figure between the ankles. As the runner measured his length on the corridor floor, his pursuers surrounded his crumpled form.

* * *

"Just look at this, Fred!" Molly stood before him brandishing the local newspaper. He peered at the banner headline: PENSIONER BRINGS DRUG-CRAZED PATIENT TO HIS KNEES.

And there he was – on the front page, surrounded by a group of pretty, smiling nurses. He liked that. Sixty years on and he hadn't quite forgotten <u>all</u> his army training!

GOING UP IN THE WORLD
Sheila Charles

WHO? A fox – that's me – Harold. WHERE? A building site, yes – but not just any building site! Yes, London's tallest building, due to be finished in 2012. They keep on going up, and each time they put in another floor, I just have to rise to it. Not so easy though without proper apples and pears, but I'm young and nimble, I've got a good head for heights and Balance is my second name. It's getting a bit windy now I'm up so high, but the view is stupendous and there's always plenty to eat. These builders really know what a fox needs to survive.

Take Jack. He takes a sarnie and *The Sun*, wanders over to the window so's he can see better – gets engrossed, forgets about his lunch. What an invitation.

Then there's Matt and his doorsteps. He eats up real quick, throws the crusts at those scavenging birds. I can soon scare them off and even catch one if I'm quick.

Charlie's my favourite though. Those chicken legs are irresistible. He never picks them clean, so I get to do that. Neither of us are keen on those jalapenos – make my eyes water – but I'm getting used to the hummus.

Well enough about food, I had a mission. I was going to meet my destiny. Father said, "We expect you to rise to great heights to meet your destiny, Harold," so, late one chilly February evening, I left the Olympic Stadium where I was born. I had my sights set on the best building site in London. I kept my nose close to the ground, my ears open and my feet clean. I stayed in the shadows while picking my way round restaurants and pubs. I gleaned information (it's an irregular triangular shape, like a shard of glass), heard rumours (the design was sketched on the back of a menu by Renzo Piano, the Italian architect), and ignored the scandal about extravagance and a world recession (it won't affect me). I passed great grandfather's resting place under the Crystal Phallus. I paid my respects before crossing the tangle of diesel-spattered tracks at Fenchurch Street Station. I skirted round The Tower in the hopes of finding some scraps of meat but was disappointed. I hurried on to Billingsgate for a fish supper, but it seems that progress or is it the recession (?) has put paid to all these good old traditions.

I still had plenty of time before dawn so I thought I'd backtrack and cross the river via Tower Bridge. (I was so relieved the Americans didn't remove it when they bought it.) According to Dad's map, once across the river I would almost be there. I heard the clock strike four as I reached the south side of the Thames. Big Ben, I realised, wasn't far downstream. I stopped for a rest, squeezing under some warped Herrell fencing encircling some bins and found some old bones. So that's where the Beefeaters hide their scraps.

I arrived at the familiar dusty noisy atmosphere of the prestigious building site before it was light and it was simple from there on – up, up and away, for I knew my destiny was at the top. It would have been much easier to use the lift, but I couldn't reach the buttons to operate it. Climbing up, step by step, was quite a feat. Dad would have been proud of me. I'd have sent him a postcard but there weren't any up there. I'd have sent him a photo but ... no camera, and he hadn't given me his address. Anyway I must keep looking forward. I'd come this far and would be able to reach the top, where my destiny would be waiting for me. I wondered where she would have travelled from and what stories she'd have to tell.

Apart from the hammering this would have made for executive living and I could see it was ideal for an ambitious family. The view was a fly runner's dream and when The Shard is finished they say it will be a positive addition to London's skyline. I also heard that foxes will have to evolve wings to live successfully at such heights. Pah!

THE ECLIPSE
Rosemary Davis

It's a cold moonlit night as I stand with my pyjamas on, a tracksuit over them, a thick coat, and then all wrapped up in a blanket, with my camera at the ready.

The time is about seven a.m., the date is 21st December 2010. As I watch the moon silently slide across the sky, an unseen monster starts to nibble into it. In fact it's the shadow of the earth as it passes between our sun and the moon, and as I take photo after photo, I wonder what our ancestors would have made of this occurrence. Now all I can see is a black orb, highlighted by a white glow.

The moon starts to reappear and within a few hours, as it dips down behind the trees, it breaks free.

WHAT YE SOW
Deborah Dunseith

The council phoned; I've got a plot. It's been so long I'd almost forgotten I was on their list. Now I'm thinking of chitting potatoes and growing Mum's favourite *Love-In-A-Mist*.

It won't be much but it's all mine. A little patch of ground soaking up my blood, sweat and tears, and when you curse nobody hears except the slugs and the dandelions.

For Mother's Day, when the children ask, I'd like a blue gingham kneeling-pad and a Thermos flask and a sturdy tin to store next year's seeds and a garden claw for pulling weeds.

I'll grow some sprouts for Christmas lunch and protect them from the *Cabbage White* who insist on laying eggs, despite my best efforts to pick them off and drown them in the water trough.

What about some ex-battery hens? I could get some wire and enlist some friends to help me make a pen. And they'll provide cheap organic manure for the compost heap.
What ye sow, so shall ye reap.

LOST
Iris Welford

It's been five years now and though I don't think about it every day, I still go over it, usually when I am in that half-world state before sleep comes.

* * *

It was a perfect day, blue skies interspersed with fleeting white clouds. We were all looking forward to our picnic on the sands as we made our way down to the beach. It was our yearly ritual. My father was holding the basket, with help from John, my eldest boy. Mum was talking to Pete, my husband, and trailing behind us was Chloe, who was in one of her "leave me alone" moods. The picture is so vivid I could paint it. Dad with his white shirt sleeves rolled up, John in his blue shorts and white trainers, Mum with her wide-brimmed sun hat, Chloe in her short red skirt and Pete with his dark glasses and denim jeans; a typical family on an August day.

John ran ahead and found a spot which was sheltered from the onshore breeze. Dad set to with Pete and put up the striped windbreak, even though it had a few holes in it, whilst Mum and I anchored the tablecloth down with stones which Chloe had rounded up. I produced plastic glasses out of the hamper and Pete opened our champagne whilst John and Chloe had Coke.

I remember Dad raised his glass and said, "Happy holidays kids – no school; and happy holiday Pete – no work; and most of all Happy Birthday Gran."

We all said, "Cheers," and hugged Mum.

A little later, Pete made us all get up to play rounders with an oversized beach ball and bat he bought at the shop on the beach road. Sand flew everywhere and Dad cheated, much to Chloe's disgust. As we were playing, a Scottie dog came along, no owner in sight, and decided to lift its leg and pee down Pete's trousers. We all howled with laughter as he chased the monster away. Game over, Mum thought it was time to eat, so we went back to get things organised and set about arranging our fold-up chairs. Dad, John and Chloe decided to go for a walk along the beach and Pete said he was going to the shop to buy a pair of shorts because he smelt of dog.

"Lunch in half an hour," I shouted as they walked off in different directions.

A few more people, mostly couples, had come on to the beach and, as the wind had eased, I decided to do a bit of sunbathing while Mum pottered around. I must have dozed off because the next thing I knew, Dad was shaking my shoulder. "Have you seen Chloe?" he asked. I could see he was worried as he was frowning.

"No, I thought she was with you. Where did you go?"

"We'd been walking for about ten minutes when Chloe said she was going back to Gran; I think she was fed up with John and me talking about football. I watched her run up one of the dunes and when she got to the top she turned and waved and we waved back. That was at least forty-five minutes ago."

I can still feel the lurch my stomach made and how I was instantly filled with panic. John, at fifteen years old, seemed to take command of the situation. He told Dad to find Pete, told me to go down to the water's edge to see if she was there, and told Gran to stay put and keep her eyes open whilst he went along the top of the dunes looking for her.

"Don't worry Mum," he said as he put his hand on my shoulder. "She may have fallen and hurt herself or something."

We went our separate ways, though I was sure Chloe was probably in the shop with Pete. Down at the water's edge there were a few people paddling, some children, a woman with a baby and that Scottie dog running around barking. I asked several of the adults if they had seen a young girl in a bright red skirt but they all shook their heads. One couple said they would keep an eye out as they strolled along the beach. I carried on searching and must have gone at least a mile in the opposite direction, but found nothing.

When I got back, the family was waiting. Pete and Dad had scoured the beach road, the shops, and the cafés and had gone back to the car park, but there was no trace. John had run along the sand dunes and had asked people if they had seen her, but still no response. Mum was very tearful and I cried too; Dad, Pete and John looked grim.

Dad looked at his watch. "It's been over two hours now, I think we must tell the police. They will let the coast-guard know, just in case she is swimming or on a li-lo or something."

It all becomes a bit of a blur now, so much happened in a short space of time. We all went to the police station where a policewoman took details from me. She asked what Chloe was wearing, how she was feeling, did she have a boyfriend; it went on and on. Pete was put in another room to answer questions and I remember feeling that the police thought we were hiding something.

Time passed with no trace of Chloe. The papers kept phoning us asking for interviews. The sea search found nothing. Police did a sweep of the beach and found her friendship bracelet – a little silver thing with half a heart on it. All the time I was trying to be positive and controlled but when the bracelet was found, I broke down. It was something Chloe would never have taken off, she treasured it.

Pete and I had to make a television appeal but people said Pete did not look upset and he knew more than he was saying.

Neighbours seemed to avoid me and shop assistants stared at us and pointed. I could read their lips when they whispered to each other, "He's guilty, I bet he killed her."

Rumours always left a seed of doubt in my mind. But my daughter had been snatched away from under my nose and I could do nothing but wait.

About two years later, we moved house. Pete lost his job. John went off to university and started a new life. Mum and Dad aged fast and we never went to the beach again. That was the day when our family died but I still hope in my heart that Chloe ran off to London or somewhere and I am waiting for the day when she can pick up the phone and say, "Hello Mum."

TOO LARGE
Hazel Gooderson

"Grandma B says it is our turn to do Christmas dinner this year."

"Oh Ben, it's the first year in our own house and I wanted it to be just the two of us on the 25th – unwrapping our presents in front of a real log fire, Christmas carols playing and champagne sparkling with the fairy lights."

"Sorry precious, perhaps we could do all that on Christmas Eve, like our Scandinavian neighbours."

That was July, and now it was December.

At the beginning of Advent, Chloe had started to plan with lists and to even look forward to the day. At least she was better off than Darcie in the office, who had to sleep all her relatives.

Together, she and Ben had gone to Thetford Forest to select a fir tree. Their Edwardian house lent itself to a large real tree to permeate the day with fresh pine. They strapped the netted parcel to the roof rack and drove carefully home, where it was unloaded and earthed into an enormous pot.

"It's too large Ben, it will never fit."

Scratched and sweating profusely, Ben wrestled with the green Norwegian symbol. He was going to make this the tree of 2010 to be photographed and remembered.

It did fit and looked splendid as it stood erect with tasteful decorations adorning its branches.

A few wrapped gifts slowly gathered at the base, but Ben's main present was too large to leave there and he would have been able to guess that Chloe had got him a racing bike.

The couple were going to have a steak and champagne supper on Christmas Eve and a four p.m. Christmas Day lunch for the immediate sixteen members of the family.

With Grandma B supplying the traditional Christmas pudding and various others contributing to the meal, it fell to Ben and Chloe to do the protein.

There had been much discussion in the Bennett household as to whose *Best Ever Christmas Day Meal* they would follow. There was the vegetarian option, or the goose like Bob Cratchit in Charles Dickens. Nigella had told them to soak the turkey in a bucket in the garage. Mrs Beeton wanted them to stuff the bird and Jamie said put it in when you go to bed. Delia's guide was to use the oven timer to click in whilst you slept and don't, whatever you do, stuff it.

The front covers of the seasonal magazines invited you to try new ways with sprouts, how to decorate your Christmas cake, and colour schemes for the festive table.

Chloe called to Ben, "How many minutes per pound, or is it kilos. What weight is Mr Turkey Lurkey?"

"It's twelve, like we discussed love." With that, the phone rang and Ben spoke into the receiver.

The beautiful plump turkey sat on the draining board where Ben had placed it after collecting it from the butcher. He had meant to get Chloe to guess how much it cost; a frozen one would have been cheaper, according to the TV adverts, but he wanted the family to comment on the tasty meat, and for Uncle Robbie to say, as always, "There's nothing like fresh, boy."

"Chloe, old Mrs Munday just wants me to pop round and help her. Won't be long."

Alone at the sink, she stroked the flesh and began preparing it for the baking tin. "I'll just leave him for Ben to lift across while I check my e-mails," she thought and she went to the desk to turn the computer on.

It was eight o'clock the following morning, when Ben lifted the beautiful bird to the pre-heated oven, that he let out an almighty screech: "It won't go in, Chloe, it's too large!"

WINTER MAGIC
Enid Scoging

Eight-thirty a.m., and an overnight frost has left its mark. The forest casts its early-morning spell.

Trudging along the pathways the silence is almost tangible – but not quite. A gentle tap, tap, tapping sound is quietly invasive. The early morning mists are settling on leaves and branches, transforming themselves into droplets of moisture which slither and slide on the wet surfaces, then fall into the dense undergrowth of brown bracken. The dying fronds are transformed into glossy lace fans.

Long straight lines of trees have become avenues of whiteness, their finger-branches reaching across each aisle. The rows of conifers reveal a glimpse into a wondrous fairyland.

Everywhere hundreds, millions, of spiders have worked their special magic, decorating trunks and branches, stems and grasses with their exquisite tracery. Fragile threads festoon bare twigs as far as the eye can see. Diamond drops glitter along every strand. No breeze disturbs this early hour, but the glistening webs quiver in the air as if a gentle breath is passing through, teasing each dainty wheel into movement, not daring to crush such ethereal beauty.

RESTLESS LEGS
Deborah Dunseith

The people-carrier, newly serviced, sits gleaming in the drive, a testament to its one careful owner.

The glove box has been duly stuffed with fruit pastilles, mint imperials and Calpol. The in-car DVD is ready to go at the push of a button. The audience need to be shown to their seats. A fruit drink, a packet of crisps, a comfy pillow and Bailey Bear for the youngest.

Suddenly panic breaks out. The camera has not been charged. The Ogre stomps about cursing, arms flailing and threatening to eat any little children who get in his way. A terrible roar echoes throughout the land. The hound has chewed the charger. It's a good job the hound has been banished to The Kennels or else she wouldn't fancy its chances.

One final push and, with military-style precision, each member exits the building with his own kit bag. Some exceed the required size ... but wait, the troops are rebelling. An iPod has been overlooked. The eldest protests, pleads, sulks and is finally allowed to re-enter the building. Objective, seek and find. Mission accomplished. At last silence. A deep breath.

RAC route map on lap, plus a well-thumbed road map of Britain just in case.

"What we don't have now, we don't need," comes the familiar battle cry. The signal to advance. The engine revs. Once more unto the breach.

* * *

Eight miles completed, only another two hundred and ten to go. The heavens open. A flurry of restless legs.

"Are we there yet Mum?"

"Here we go again," she thought.

HOT PICKINGS
Margaret Dutton

"Le Vendange! When? Demain. Huit heures! OK! See you then." Tim rushed out to say we had been asked to join Jules and Marcelle's grape-picking.

"So they must think of us as real neighbours, not just summer visitors. But, eight o'clock! Is there such a time in France? And we're invited to the meal when it is all done. Fantastic, eh? I'll bring the cine-camera; I feel really accepted, and proud."

Next morning we drove to the misty vineyard that clung down the steep slope of our neighbours' land, in the lovely Lot Valley. Dusty Citroëns, Renaults and Peugeots were already parked under trees. Jules had everyone in place at eight o'clock, and the picking began on the dot. Family, neighbours, cousins, friends were allocated a row, along with huge plastic buckets and fierce secateurs. Immediately they tore into the vines, pulling off leaves, and throwing the grapes into the buckets. We gingerly faced each other over our vine row and started to pick, not exactly one by one, à la 'Margot' from *The Good Life*, but we only chose the best-looking grapes. Our picking companions rapidly left us behind, and soon Jules came alongside us in his tractor.

"Non, non!" he roared, jumping down from the cab. "Comme ci, like this," and he cut bunch after bunch, including stems, mildewed shrivelled grapes and threw everything into the bucket. Thoroughly shamed, we took up the challenge, working harder than ever. Buckets filled, ready to be hauled up into the slowly moving trailer, we gradually moved up our row. Aching arms, legs and faces became sticky with grape juice, dust, sweat and flies, and we dared not stop to film anything. No one talked, a few whistled, everyone had a sense of urgency. The dreamy French rural picture became a nightmare. Bleeding dirty blisters developed on our hands, the sun was relentless on our bent backs. Not one picker stopped other than for a call of nature, discreetly behind a stripped row, and facing downhill.

After four gruelling hours the tractor made its last journey back to Jules' small farm; exhausted and filthy we staggered down to our Mini. Pouring water we had brought into a bowl, we soaped away some of the grime, combed out the dust and cobwebs and changed into fresh T-shirts and jeans.

"How much did we pick?" asked Tim wearily. "I lost count after thirty-three buckets, but I know they weigh fifty kilograms loaded! This had better be the most delicious wine, ever."

We were surprised on two counts as we sat down under the shady trees for the magnificent lunch of home produced ham, patés, poached fish, cheeses, and bowls of soft-skinned peaches and raspberries. Out of thirty pickers, we were the *only ones* who had washed and changed; and on the tables were dozens of fine chateaux-bottled Bordeaux wines. Not one bottle of home produced wine to be seen.

"Bien sûr, of course, only the best for my vendange friends!" smiled Jules filling our polished glasses. "But today's production will be bottled and waiting for you when you come back next year. Merci, et bon appetit!"

A DAY OUT
Enid Scoging

A week off work, away from the factory with all its noisy machinery, away from the smells and clatter of the canteen – Norah Hastings savoured the thought as she plunged her strong arms into the wash-tub. She brushed her hair from her brow with her forearm as the steam rose from the pile of shirts. She scrubbed at the collars and cuffs with brush and soap, dreaming of the day when Alf would keep his promise to buy her one of them new-fangled electric wash-tubs.

As she scrubbed, she thought again of the poster advertising the Works' Outing. It had been on the factory notice-board for weeks. Its bold lettering had enticed her each time she passed by. There had been a similar one in the canteen close to the till where she sat each day.

Norah liked her job. It was better than being on the factory floor. But – it had its drawbacks. Sitting still, perched on a hard seat, day in, day out, she noticed the inches increasing, especially round her middle and bum. Still, Alf always said that he liked his women well-covered. She also wondered from time to time just how many women he had liked. But they never, ever, talked about things like that. Not much time really with six kids to bring up. Only young Billy at home now. After National Service he had got a job at the factory, too, working in the warehouse.

The back door swung open and Billy's cheery voice greeted her: "Hello, Mum. What's for tea?"

Norah dried her hands and reached for the kettle. "Where's yer Dad?" she asked as the water spurted.

"In the Nag's Head. Said he'd be home later."

Norah sighed and gritted her teeth. Another battle over Alf's pay-packet was looming. Still, she had something to look forward to. The Works' Outing was advertised as a mystery tour. Alf and Billy were booked on it, too. Norah was convinced the attraction lay in all the coach stops, both going and coming, when convenient dashes to pub lavatories or road-side bushes were preceded by the odd pint – or two! Norah poured the boiling water on the tea leaves, replaced the lid and waited for the brew to mash.

The day of the Works' Outing arrived. Four green and white charabancs were lined up at the factory gates. Everybody looked different. Gone were the overalls and boiler-suits. Gone were the aprons and head scarves. The older men wore their best suits and trilby hats. Younger men were more casual, probably rebelling after the years spent in uniform. The women wore the best clothes they could muster by saving their clothing coupons.

Norah heaved herself up the steps of the first green and white 'chara' and inched her bulk along the aisle to a seat by a window. Alf followed, hat in hand, newspaper in pocket. Billy, she noticed, settled himself beside that pretty young Rita from Accounts. She was smiling and giggling.

"Hmm," thought Norah, nudging Alf in the ribs and pointing.

The four fully-loaded charabancs moved off in convoy and wound their way through the busy city streets. It was Wakes Week. Factory and office workers were out and about experiencing the freedom of their annual holiday. Theirs were not the only vehicles escaping the confines of brick and concrete.

Out in the countryside, Norah enjoyed the greenness of trees and shrubs and open fields. The warm sun shone from a blue sky through the window and on to her face. She felt herself relaxing. She leaned back and closed her eyes. Alf didn't want to talk. He had his nose in the *Racing Times*, studying form again. Perhaps – one day – he'd win a fortune and that new washing-machine would be hers. The churning and throbbing of the coach wheels almost sounded like her heart's desire. Alf had promised, hadn't he? But somehow, all too often, York's racecourse and the Nag's Head ate into the pounds and the pennies. But today, away from the city, the factory, the washing, the cooking, Norah was gong to enjoy the mystery outing.

The flapping of the newspaper disturbed her.

"Wake up, old girl. Nearly there."

With a startled snort Norah turned her head to peer through the window, and her heart sank as she read the large signpost looming by the roadside: DONCASTER RACECOURSE – FOLLOW THE SIGNS.

AN UPLIFTING MOMENT
Rosemary Ford

Mirror, mirror on the wall.
Why don't you make me thin and tall?

My dear, my dear, it can't be done;
If you appear as short and fat,
There's nothing I can do 'bout that.
But don't you know it's up to you
To eat much less and walk more too?

I know, I know, I know you're right.
I will try hard, I'll fight and fight.
I'll eat one biscuit, then I'll walk
Right down to town, not stop and talk.
I'll go to SHE, that nice wee shop,
And buy a bra to give a lift,
And e'en perhaps a girdle new –
That's sure to make a difference too.
Then mirror, mirror please be kind,
Or else a new one I'll have to find.

SISTERLY JEALOUSY
Hazel Gooderson

"Listen to this postcard from my sister: *Breakfast and lunch al fresco on our terrace. Reading under the palm trees and swimming in the Med daily.* And here *we* are, looking out at grey skies. It should have been me that Clive married. I saw him first. Now don't get me wrong, Tom, I do love you but you haven't given me the financial security Simone has had."

It was eleven o'clock on a Saturday in September. The beautiful raven-haired Jackie was ready to do her weekly visit to their mother. She pulled on her knee-length boots and buttoned herself into the woollen jacket. Tom watched her from the comfort of his cat basket.

Jackie walked the short distance to her mother's house, the wind whipping around her slender frame.

"Hi Mum, shall I put the kettle on? Had a card this morning from Simone and Clive. I thought they should be back by now. Why, whatever has happened, you look terrible? Oh, hello Clive, what are you doing here? I didn't notice your car."

"Clive arrived just before you. It's your sister. She's in intensive care. I need to go to her bedside, Jackie."

"Yes of course Mum, I'll come with you."

Apart from their shoes echoing along the hospital corridor, not a word was spoken amongst the three concerned relatives. They reached the room where Clive had briefly left his wife.

"Only one visitor at a time, Mr Martin, but she has been asking for Jackie," the mid-thirties, plump, pink-cheeked nurse said in a low voice.

Clive turned to his sister-in-law. "You'd better go first then."

Simone turned her head from the hospital bed towards the opening door. A drip was feeding her hand which lay on top of the sheet. She tried to smile.

"Oh Jackie, I think I'm going to die and I needed to ask your forgiveness before I do. All my life I've been jealous of you, my older sister. You are so pretty and you have had a child. We've been told that I'll never have any. You have all the brains and Mum has always loved you more."

Jackie looked at her sister. Now was the time for her to confess, and she was not on her deathbed.

"All my life I've been jealous of you Simone – your devoted husband and sense of fun, the numerous holidays and friends."

Their mother peered through the window in the door and saw her two beautiful daughters with tears rolling down their cheeks. She loved them both so dearly; she hoped the doctors could save her little Simone so they could comfort one another when her time came to depart.

WEATHER OR NOT
Rosemary Davis

"Duncan, shall we have a barbecue tomorrow and invite a few friends? You've worked so hard on the garden and it looks so pretty, it'll be a shame not to show it off."

"Yes, that sounds like a great idea. I'll go and ring round to see who can come."

Duncan disappears into the other room, as Diana starts to make a list. She can hear him chatting on the phone. When he reappears he says, "Twenty definite, but you know what Jenny's like – can't make a decision with out first clearing it with the weatherman, Jamie, and her horoscope."

Diana laughs. "Is Jethro coming?"

"Yes, why?"

"Well if he's coming, Jenny will be here, even if it floods and Mercury is at war with Venus."

Duncan looks at his wife of twenty-two years and raises his straight black eyebrows.

"If we get twenty-four of every thing, that will be plenty," she continues.

Bending slightly, he puts his arm round her waist. "Twenty-four lettuces seems a bit excessive."

Her elbow comes back catching him squarely in the ribs as she says, "You know what I mean."

He goes, "Ouch," and while laughing he goes to get the car.

* * *

Next morning they work hard getting the barbecue ready for lighting, the chairs and table out and the gazebo up. By mid-afternoon everyone had arrived except for Jenny. With the party in full swing and music, laughter, jokes and dancing, no one took any notice of the black clouds rolling in, until there's an almighty clap of thunder and big drops of rain start to pepper everything. Everyone starts to disappear inside but the party continues as the rain lashes down outside. Over the noise Diana hears the door bell and opens it to a very bedraggled Jenny, with rivulets of rain running down her face from her usually pristine hair. Duncan appears at this moment and says, "What did you say yesterday Diana?"

And they both burst into laughter as they usher a very bemused Jenny into the kitchen to get her dry.

THE PEEP SHOW
Sheila Charles

Flo was the eldest of the three ageing sisters. They usually met up every Thursday for lunch, but since John had started working nights she got bored. So this week Flo invited them over for the evening instead. She had a real 'peep show' for them tonight and the sandwiches and the whiskey, would help the evening go with a swing.

Betty and Ellen arrived as the clock struck eight thirty p.m. Their curiosity was roused by the lateness of the hour, but the sight of the bright red lacy knickers and a pair of black silk boxers shorts abandoned half way up the stairs was even more exciting. The excessive amount of lipstick round Flo's mouth confirmed she was on form.

The air of excitement and anticipation rose further when Flo said, "You'll never guess what I've found. Wait here for a moment. I'll call you when I'm ready."

She disappeared into the back room and from the rustling, rattling noises they knew she was rummaging through the old chest, where she kept all her private things under lock and key.

"I wonder what kind of peep show she's got for us this time? Do you remember that bloke with the purple feather boa last month?" whispered Betty.

"Ooh girls, come in here – just look at this – it's amazing," shouted Flo. "What do you make of this?"

Betty looked at Ellen and raised an eyebrow. They waddled through as quickly as their swollen legs would go. Jostling for position, Ellen squeezed through the narrow doorway, just in front of Betty, and noticed a bright flash as Flo switched off the light.

"Oh, whatever is it?" said Betty, looking towards the forty-two inch flat screen in front of the large picture window.

"Don't you ever draw your curtains Flo?" Ellen chuckled.

"What is that! It's huge," said Betty, moving nearer the telly to get a closer look.

"I'm not sure – I've never seen anything like it before," said Flo, with a bemused smile creeping across her wrinkled jaw. And there they stood, with their hands over their mouths in utter disbelief of what they could see.

"It's got a strange glow to it, hasn't it?" Ellen said, rearranging her glasses to get a better view.

Betty moved over to the TV, watching quietly. Every now and then she pointed and gasped, taking yet another swig of whiskey. Without her knowing, Flo kept topping up her glass and she and Ellen just giggled at her gasps of bewilderment. She had always been gullible, innocent and naïve. Of course she had never married, never crossed the borders of Norfolk, even.

"It's all making me feel dizzy," said Betty after a while. She'd never been able to stomach anything too strong or unnatural!

"*Wild Turkey* is very strong, you know, Flo?" muttered Ellen.

"Yeah, but it was on offer."

"Oh, good heavens, what's going on now?" Betty cried as she took another peep at the show.

"Ooh yes. It's getting even bigger and it's changing colour!" Ellen had a sharp eye for detail.

"I don't think I can take anymore, I feel rather sick. This whiskey doesn't agree with me. It's late as well. I think I'll call a taxi if you don't mind," said Betty, looking rather flushed.

"Oh, come on Bets, you'll be all right. I know it's rather strange but it's different, don't you think? I thought you'd be interested and it's not something I'll ever show you again, I promise." She winked at Ellen who had finished her whiskey and was happily supping Betty's unwanted remains.

Flo continued to reassure Betty as Ellen drew the curtains and switched the light back on. She was enjoying the evening; she had no intention of leaving yet. She poured herself another whiskey. It was smoky and ran so smoothly over her tongue as she rolled it round her mouth. Betty eventually stopped fidgeting and looked round for her glass.

"Where's mine?" she demanded. "I think I need a big one after all that and then I'll be off."

"Oh don't go just yet, I've made us some sandwiches and we must arrange our Christmas outing," said Flo, offering her the plate on which three sandwiches were carefully arranged divided by three pieces of lettuce.

"Now come on, help me eat these up, dear, and then tell us where you fancy going this year. Are you up for the Chippendales this time?"

Flo stood at the door waving her sisters goodbye and none of them heard Big Ben chiming to herald the start of *News at Ten*, or the explanation of the peep show the three sisters had been watching in the night sky.

"The first sighting of Halley's Comet for over one hundred years has been watched by delighted thousands, thanks to a cloudless night."

MOTHER'S PRAYER
Margaret Dutton

Oh Lord, please help to make me smile
For I'm about to lose my child
And be a mother-in-law.

The baby I bounced on my knee
Who sucked his thumb 'til he was three
Doesn't need me anymore.

The pretty girl who has arrived
And stands beside him side by side
Will take my place for evermore.

And in this place, this sunny day
I have to give him all away
My heart is grieving and so sore.

But then they turn and smile at me
And place a present on my knee
My tears won't hold back and they pour.

Inside the box is one gold heart
Inscribed with "You will be a part
of me, and your new daughter-in-law."

So, thank you Lord, you helped me smile
I've gained a daughter, kept my child,
And soon, I hear, there will be more!

DO YOU FANCY A HOLIDAY?
Hazel Gooderson

Flying used to be quite a pleasant pastime. But all that stopped on September 11th 2001.

Special offers, discounts, sales and one-time-only deals tempt us on the internet; what rubbish. £1 to our destination, £100 back; add airport taxes, extra for a cardboard meal, extra for luggage, extra to book the seat.

Sometimes our suitcase may have gone a couple of kilos over and we are forced to pay excess, or unpack around the corner to hand-carry the offending two kilos. But the smug, morbidly obese person in the queue behind with just his passport and wallet walks through. Nobody asks him to get on the scales and pay for each additional kilo he is carrying around his middle that, in a couple of hours, will be spilling over his seat and armrest onto ours (when he has only paid for one).

Now, not only do we have to go through the humiliating experience of a virtual strip search (coats off, boots off, belts off, jewellery off, pockets emptied) and X-ray, we have to watch nursing mothers being forced to drink their own expressed and bottled breast milk to prove to the Customs Officer that it doesn't contain liquid explosives, and suffer the squeals and tantrums of toddlers who are made to hand over their half-consumed cartons of apple juice because they contain more than 100ml of suspicious-looking, honey-coloured liquid that could spell the end of us all at thirty-five thousand feet.

Why do we have to stuff all our hand luggage into one bag in order to conform to the 'one bag per person' policy, but once on the other side we are allowed to spend unlimited amounts of money on various purchases and walk away from the duty-free shop with four or five carrier bags of merchandise, and nobody once says, "I'm sorry, but you've bought too many things from our shop and you cannot take that many shopping bags on to the aircraft."?

And all that is before we even take off!!!

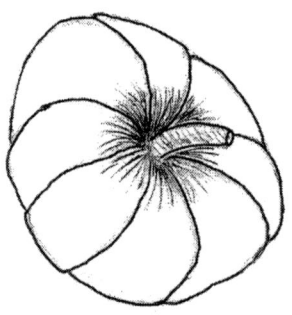

WATERSHED
Iris Welford

"This is a watershed for the United States," the news reporter droned. "People want the President to act before anything else happens to our beloved country."

I turned off the television. The scene of devastation and destruction was vivid in my mind; was it the beginning of war? My son still had no news of his wife. She worked for Morgan Grenfell on the one hundredth floor. Her job was everything to her while Mitch stayed at home doing his veterinary work in our small town. I watched that tower crumble. There was no hope for vibrant Helen; this was 9/11.

A WHOLE LOTTO LUCK
Deborah Dunseith

Laura knew that the Scottish syndicate had done the right thing by not requesting any publicity.

"Hol deet hiya," hissed Katja.

Laura duly raised her corner of the giant cheque, fixed her sweetest smile and waited for the cameras to start flashing.

The press had wanted them to pose in their coffee shop uniforms but Katja had said, "Balls to that," in her broken English and had taken the opportunity instead to show off her impressive new cleavage in a tiny, cerise, clingy top and matching skimpy shorts that left absolutely nothing to the imagination.

It had been an easy decision for Laura to hand in her notice despite recently winning the much sought-after 'Employee of the Year' award for excellence in hot beverages and for making a 'flat white' to Mr Lafayette's exacting standards. Now that she was a millionairess the world was her oyster. Mr Lafayette had been furious at the mass exit of his staff, especially his head barista. "Serves him right," thought Laura. Instead of laughingly pointing out the very slim chances of winning the jackpot, he should have supported his staff and joined the syndicate. 'Monsieur tight-arse' the others called him behind his back.

She wondered what Mehmet from the chip shop would say about her wonderful win. He'd recently tried to impress her with his deep-fried Mars bars but they'd not really caught on round here. She did quite fancy him though and maybe it was time to take him up on his offer of a date. As she rounded the corner she was surprised to see that the 'Golden Cod' was closed. Lunchtime was one of Mehmet's busiest periods and it was never closed at this time. Perhaps they had gone back to Istanbul. Mehmet had said that one of his uncles was ill. Perhaps he had died?

Laura caught the number twenty-seven home. The bus stopped right outside the two up, two down in Kensal Rise she shared with her mum.

"Oh Laura love," her mum enthused, "I saw you on the lunchtime news. I think I pressed record at the right time. You looked so lovely on TV but then I always said you were photogenic. Dad would have been proud. I bet he is looking down right now with a big smile on his face."

The win couldn't have come at a better time after a difficult few years. Laura knew a lovely holiday somewhere hot would be just the tonic her mum needed. What better than an extravagant cruise? Mum had always liked the sound of that.

"You're in luck," smiled the overly-made-up travel agent, glancing at her colleague and thinking of all the commission. "There is one superior luxury suite available on the Ocean Vista departing Southampton next Thursday. Would you like me to go ahead and book your dream cruise to the Canary Islands?"

"Thank you Vanessa," said Laura peering at the girl's name badge. "I just can't wait!"

Laura and her mum spent the rest of the week shopping for cruise-wear in London's poshest designer outlets. They hired personal shoppers to gather elegant silk evening gowns, hottest trend heels and Swarovski crystal-encrusted bikinis whilst they quaffed pink champagne and nibbled canapés like A-list celebrities. They pampered themselves with luxurious spa treatments at The Sanctuary in Covent Garden and even tried the latest Kangal fish pedicures in the trendy Fulham Road. They lunched at Simpsons of the Strand and dined at eight at The Ivy and Le Gavroche. The high-life certainly seemed to suit them, but

Laura couldn't help thinking of Mehmet. The fish and chip shop had now been closed for days with no sign of life from within.

The day of the cruise dawned. A shiny silver, chauffeur-driven limousine arrived to escort them to Southampton. The brand new Louis Vuitton luggage was placed reverently in the huge boot and the driver showed the two delighted women how to operate the state-of-the-art in-car entertainment and the well-stocked cocktail bar. By the time they arrived at the docks Laura and her mum were beside themselves with glee, riding high on a wave of excited expectancy.

"Welcome aboard the Ocean Vista," announced the dashing young Captain as Laura and her mum made their way on board.

"This is going to be amazing love," said Laura's mum hugging her daughter.

After a quick unpacking session and freshen-up, the pair click-clacked their way to the Blue Lagoon Bar to read the cruise overview brochure and plan their many excursions.

"Oooh, look Mum, there's a musical on tonight after dinner, or perhaps you'd like to try your luck in the casino?"

"I am lucky love, lucky to have a smashing daughter like you." Her mum's eyes filled with tears. "It's just a shame your dad isn't here to enjoy it with us."

The sumptuous meal consisted of five courses. They sat with two other couples, a retired officer and his wife from Devon and two elderly sisters from Kent. The conversation was stilted at first but the copious amounts of alcohol soon loosened tongues.

"Dorothy thinks she recognises you from the television," ventured one of the sisters to Laura.

"Oh yes," Laura's mum was quick to interject, winking at Laura, "my daughter's famous all right!"

"Could I have your autograph for my friend's son? He made a fortune selling a signed copy of Alan Titchmarsh's latest novel on eBay."

The musical hit all the right notes but Laura's mum was beginning to flag.

"You go and enjoy yourself with the young ones love and I'll see you back at the suite," she said handing Laura her key-card.

"Maybe I'll just go up to the next deck and see if I can find the disco," Laura kissed her mum goodnight and called the glass lift in the main atrium.

The lift doors opened to a cacophony of sound. "Welcome to The Spanish Experience," a young waitress shouted above the noise. "Would you like some sangria?" Laura helped herself to a glass and drank it down rather too quickly. The heady atmosphere and the addictive Latin beat made her sway to the rhythm and it wasn't long before she was grabbed by a young man resplendent in fluorescent green Hawaiian shirt and shorts.

"Wanna do the Lambada?" he breathed, his face partly obscured beneath a huge flapping sombrero.

Twice round the deck they danced, treading on each other's feet, as the music got louder and the pace got hotter. Laura's moist palms slipped constantly from her partner's but were firmly directed back into place. She felt her head spinning but it was wonderful to be lost in the moment, tightly pressed against this muscular and energetic young man.

Her partner suddenly spun her around, grabbed her by the waist and pulled her close to him. His hand rose slowly to tip off the sombrero revealing a familiar cheeky grin.

"Mehmet," cried Laura overjoyed to see her lost beau.

"We won the Lotto," shrieked Mehmet sweeping Laura off her feet and twirling her around and around.

"You won the Lotto too?"

"My family in Glasgow shared the rollover jackpot with your coffee shop. We saw you on TV, by the way, and my cousin said you looked a bit of all right."

Laura flushed.

"We must have booked this cruise at the same time as you," continued Mehmet. "Wasn't that lucky?"

"Oh yes," said Laura kissing Mehmet full on the lips. "Very lucky indeed!"

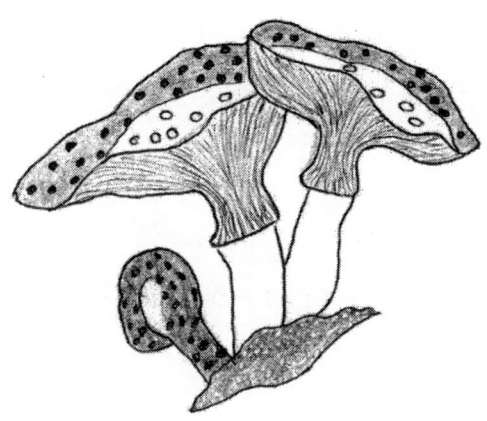

WIND
Enid Scoging

Tall stately poplars
Swayed drunkenly,
Their tops teased into motion
By a gentle wind.
Leaves brushed together,
Shushing and sighing.
Beneath them the denser bushes
Clustered like great green clouds
Their branches catching the sunlight
And writhing with summer pleasure.
The wind was persistent,
Encouraging movement
In every direction.

WELCOME TO ATTLEBOROUGH
Rosemary Ford

Regor Drof woke with a start as the coach pulled up at a brightly-lit place. He had tried so hard to stay awake and take in all the sights of this new country. The journey had been long and the arrival at Heathrow terrifying with its hustle and pushing and confusion. But he had managed to find the bus station and buy a ticket to the town where Lehcar was waiting with a flat and a job. Strange name this town had. He had it written down to show the disinterested woman at the ticket office: 'ATTLEBOROUGH'.

"Get the bus marked Norwich," she muttered when he asked which way to go. That was all right because Lehcar had written that name down for him as well. Everyone seemed to be walking in different directions pulling huge cases and bags. Regor had all he possessed in one black bag with the handle hanging off and he had to drag it along. Soon he would buy a smart new case, he resolved.

"Stay awake," he had ordered himself. But sleep had overtaken him and here they were at this brightly-lit place. Could this be Attleborough? He must not miss his stop. He lurched to the front of the coach and asked a man, "Is this Attleborough?"

"No mate. It's Stansted Airport," replied the man with a laugh. Such a bright, shining city it looked in the darkness.

He had no idea how long his journey to his new home would take so he dare not risk sleeping again. He had finished eating the cake Mamoushka had given him. Hunger helped him stay alert. Soon the view changed to trees and fields. Could he have missed his destination? He decided to try to ring Lehcar again. He had tried many times but there had been no reply. This time he heard his friend's familiar voice replying in his own dear, familiar language. Relief!

"The bus gets here at two o'clock," said his old friend. "Meet you? Not possible. Tomorrow I must work and tonight I must sleep. Just get off the bus at Queen's Square. Turn right and right again and my flat is half-way along the road. I will leave it unlocked and the light on. Such things are possible here."

The coach sped along almost empty roads now, stopping at dark stops here and there. Then at last, just after two o'clock the bus drew up.

"Attleborough," called out the driver.

Regor stumbled to the doorway.

"This is Queen's Square?" he asked in disbelief. It was dark and steady rain was falling. He had pictured somewhere like Buckingham Palace with such a grand name.

He stumbled down the steps and collected his bag. He was excited at the prospect of his new life, but just for a few moments in the darkness he wished he had never come. He walked down a dark road and then … miraculously, a dear familiar sign appeared: 'LIDL'. Just like at home. And there, walking towards him with arms outstretched, was Lehcar.

"Welcome to Attleborough," he called. And suddenly everything was all right.